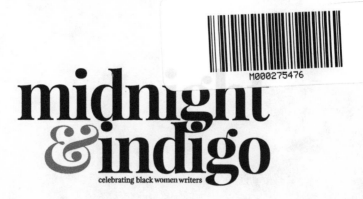

midnight & indigo
celebrating black women writers

Issue 5

EDITED BY:
Ianna A. Small

midnight & indigo
PUBLISHING

midnight & indigo

VOLUME 1, ISSUE 5
978-1-7328917-8-4

midnightandindigo.com

———————

MANUSCRIPTS AND SUBMISSIONS
Whether you've already been published or are just starting out, we want to hear from you! We accept submissions of short stories and narrative essays written by Black women writers. View complete submission guidelines and submit your stories online at *midnightandindigo.com*. No paper submissions please.

Cover image: Alexander Kozlovich/Stocksy United

Printed and bound in the United States of America.
First Printing August 2021

"I am the daughter of Black writers who are descended from freedom fighters, who broke their chains and changed the world. They call me."

~ Amanda Gorman

midnight & indigo

celebrating black women writers

ISSUE 5

Editor's Note

Like the characters in its stories, this issue was born of tenacity, grit, and patience that extends far beyond its pages.

Running a literary journal is not for the faint-hearted! Holding steady to your dream amid a global pandemic is now truly among the great wonders of the world! Persevering toward a vision is hard. Navigating through setbacks and setups, anxiety over the pace at which the goal comes to fruition, and empowering ourselves with the superpower of flexibility...each is key to growth.

Today and every day, we live in awe of the writers, authors, essayists, and poets who allow themselves the vulnerability and resolve to share their stories with the world.

We can because you do. And for that, we are eternally grateful.

In this collection, we meet characters across ages and continents, in various stages of becoming. From women who revisit and redefine their definitions of love, and young girls at the precipice of finding their place in world and family, to narrators discovering self, and sometimes, sacrifice, we are proud to present fifteen new short stories written by Black women storytellers.

In **"The Last Time"** by Wandeka Gayle, a Jamaican woman returns home for a visit from graduate school in Louisiana. She has a chance encounter with a recent ex, with whom she has had a decade-long affair.

When Chiwetalu leaves Nigeria to live the American Dream, in **"Limbo"** by Adaora Raji, he thrusts his wife into an uncertainty that stretches the boundaries of her love and loyalty. She embarks on her own journey of self-discovery.

In **"The Tractor"** by Theresa Sylvester, a single woman discovers a secret involving her pretty, married, younger sister and their vocal mother. Set in Lusaka, the story explores farm life, family bonds, and societal norms.

"Phantom Itch" by Melie Ekunno tells of the sexual struggles of a "Chibok Girl" in America. Given the kidnapping of over two hundred high school girls from their boarding school in Chibok, Nigeria in 2014 and the eventual state-sanctioned scholarships to the U.S. granted to the rescued or escaped girls, and the predominance of Female Genital Mutilation (FGM) in the region, the story explores the resulting unique psychological dissonance and trauma.

"**The Orphan's Daughter**" by Leslie D. Rose is a retelling of stories told to her by her mother, who was orphaned as a young girl in 1950s Spanish Harlem. Found with her two siblings in a small apartment, the three were taken to an orphanage on Staten Island where life as they knew it would be no more. She now knows her mother's stories to be PTSD, but the way she reflected upon her life was so majestic, they had to be retold.

Colorism in the Caribbean is examined through the lens and family history of a young Trinidadian woman and her complicated relationship with her grandmother, in "**Bittersweet**" by Melissa A. Matthews. It explores the nuances by which its legacy is passed down from generation to generation.

In "**Things I Can't Outrun**" by Amani-Nzinga Jabbar, Nakisha is a former track star who stopped running after dropping out of a mostly white college. She tries to return to her passion by registering for a charity race, an experience tainted by microaggressions. She later learns of the shooting death of a young Black jogger and realizes there are some things you just can't run from, no matter how fast you are.

Flint, Amara, and their neighbor, Ebony, spend their time with adventure and imagination, as only children can, in "**Barricade**" by Desi Lenc. One day, Ebony and Amara create a new game.

Mel's therapist seeks to save her from the despair a name brings, in "**Mel needs a new name**" by Martins Favour.

After Sadie loses her daddy one year, her mama has to go away for a while too, in "**Too Much of Anything Can Kill You**" by Ashanti Hardy. That year, Sadie learns that too much of anything can kill you.

Middle school is tough. In "**Spirit Week**" by Emily Capers, follow the narrator through her first taste of middle school Spirit Week, where she learns about spooky school rumors. For the first time, it's brought to her attention that she doesn't look quite like the rest of her peers.

In "**Free Falling**" by Adrian Joseph, Nia journeys through the darkness of her psyche, using everything within to overcome her fears and release her sinister past. Will she make it out alive?

A girl lives with the psychological trauma received during a religious experience, in **"Salvation"** by Stephanie Avery.

Lee is thrust into a caregiver role for her two younger sisters following her father's death, in **"Water Bearers"** by Danielle Buckingham. As her mother's grief consumes her, Lee is troubled with strange dreams.

"She (A retelling of *The Giving Tree*)" by rebekah blake is a retelling, but also a story about a Black mother. She gives until she has nothing left.

If you're interested in reading additional stories and essays, please check out previous issues, visit us at midnightandindigo.com, and follow us on social @midnightandindigo. Thank you for your support. Enjoy!

The Last Time

You stand at the top of the lane waiting for Warren to appear around the bend, the blood surging at your temples. You've come back to the island and, of course, had no intention of seeing him, but there you are, digging the tips of your flats into the gravel and waiting for this man.

Yesterday's words still ring in your head.

You had spotted him at the entrance of the Tastee's shop in LOJ mall the day before, hand on his phone, eyes moving from you to the man that had come to sit with you at the food court, and when you had gone over to Warren, he ignored you like you were a fly buzzing around his head, one insignificant enough to not even be swatted away.

He called you a few hours later. You heard the worry in his voice when he asked who the man was, and the exasperation when you said he was a high school friend you had run into on this visit home. Then came anger when you said there was no reason he should care anymore.

"Well, you need to get your paintings before you go back. I don't want them in my house!"

So, you have come.

He soon appears around the corner in that t-shirt, the one with the print of a child he'd painted, her face frozen in a grin expressing a joy that neither of you have shared in a long time. You hold his gaze, wondering how you could have spent the last two years in this limbo with him.

You tell yourself you are done this time.

This is the last time you will see him.

He seems taller, gaunt even. How had you let him wrap those thin arms around you? How had you let him kiss your neck, your lips, your stomach? He isn't handsome, you think, not really, but you cannot deny how the high arches of his cheekbones are beautiful even in a man.

Is he eating? Does he have enough?

You close your eyes for a moment. No. You are only there to collect your paintings and nothing else.

He stands before you now, beads of sweat on his brow from the July heat and his walk from the tenement.

"Hi," he says simply.

"Hi," you say.

"You have to come with me," he says. He shifts his weight from one foot to the other.

"I don't really want to go in," you say, looking back at the gravel road and the modest one-floor concrete houses behind zinc fences on the hill. You have only felt unease entering this community, this garrison with ever-watchful residents sure to have firepower for what they call frequent police persecution, but you know there is another threat. You remember how cool his sheets feel under your bare skin.

"Suit yourself," he says, but doesn't move. He is looking at your necklace, the one you got as a replacement when you stopped the monthly payments on an engagement ring. It has two hearts interlaced. You slip it inside the high neck of your dress but don't miss the twitch at his temples.

"How long you here for?" he asks.

"Two more days," you say.

"Well, how you going to get them if you don't come now?"

You stand there for a moment. You think about the edict of the past two years you had both made, the one that says that to remain in each other's lives you would only be friends. You could not be lovers.

"They already off the wall and everything," he says.

"Then why you didn't bring them?" you ask, but he has already started to walk away.

"Okay, fine," you say, following him down the path.

You have taken this path several times with him, but then you went away to graduate school in Louisiana. The phone calls were earnest and frequent in the beginning. When you talked, the want thick in your voices, you subsisting on memories and words for a time, until the thing could not sustain itself without the contact zones of your bodies.

You pass the bend where you'd fallen over a rock years before and he'd carried you the rest of the way, blaming your heaviness on all the mangoes you were eating one summer, swearing you would give him a hernia with the strain.

You would learn that summer you were carrying his child and then you would lose it almost just as quickly.

You walk in silence now, he two steps ahead. You wonder if he thinks about that too every time he passes that rock.

Then you feel the first raindrops and he stops.

"Come, we have to hurry," he says and extends his hand to you.

You take it without thinking and you both run through the drizzle over the uneven red earth. His grip is firm and familiar. You like how your palms are flush against each other and, as the rains come harder, how he grips your fingers tighter. You race through the narrow passage leading to this gate where he'd painted a scene of Fort Clarence beach, backdrop to your reunions and goodbyes.

Inside, you see he has planted more since you went away. The banana trees stretch almost as tall as his six-foot frame and the neat rows of bok choy now have larger foliage.

"We been waiting on some rain," he says when you make it, breathless and soaked, to the porch. He is actually smiling, his whole face lit up as he watches the welcome downpour on his patches of crops. Oddly, it is raining through intermittent rays of sunlight.

"Look like the devil and him wife at war again," he says, with a chuckle, and goes inside.

His easel has been set up with a fresh canvas and already has the outline of a stippled house and poinciana tree. You try not to think about the time he painted you while you slept naked in his bed just two days after your first meeting at that art festival.

"Let me go for a towel," he says when you step inside.

You slip out of your wet flats and pad around. You stop at the picture of him and the little girl with the same dark skin and pronounced cheekbones. You feel a pang and move away from the frame.

The colors in the room are vibrant greens and yellows and reds. You see his touches everywhere—the hand-painted vines climbing up the walls, the earthen pots and hanging enamel cups off the kitchenette, each with their own designs.

Warren comes bounding in with a towel.

"Here," he says, but instead of handing it to you, he rubs it vigorously over your short curls and your forehead. He smells the same—citrus and hard wood and oil paint.

When you look up at him, he furrows his brow.

"What happened to your locs?" he asks.

"I didn't like them. Too much work," you say.

"You should grow them back," he says, then steps back and peels off his wet t-shirt. He has let the hair grow wild on his chest, you notice, but look away.

"Give me your dress. I'll put it behind the fridge to dry," he says.

"That's... that's okay," you say. "I'm not staying long."

The sound of the rain pummeling the roof intrudes.

"You remember how you get sick running away from me into the rain? You want a repeat of that?" he says.

"You gave me your cold is what I remember," you say.

"I will turn around," he says.

You stand there awkwardly looking at the back of his head. The chiffon maxi dress is clinging to you, the lining cold and clammy against your skin.

"Okay, just bring me something to wear first."

When he leaves the room, you pull the dress over your head. Then, you look down at how the thin material of the brassiere clings to you, outlining your nipples, and you cover yourself with both hands. He's seen all of you a hundred times and the last time you'd been there he almost did again if that woman hadn't come by with his child. You try not to think of it.

He comes back with the white t-shirt with the print of the Rio Cobre painting you'd seen him create. He takes the dress from you and puts it on the heating rack behind the fridge. You turn your back to him and pull the shirt over your head. You can feel him watching you and you stop midway. In two steps, he is behind you to help you pull it down.

"You hate me?" he says.

"What?"

"I couldn't stand it if you hate me now," he says, hands stilling at your sides. "I was a jackass to you on the phone yesterday. I'm so sorry, Marcy."

You close your eyes. You hate when he calls you this pet name. When he calls you "Marcella," it feels like a rebuke. When he calls you "Marcy," something warm curdles inside you.

You turn around and look at him.

"I do hate you," you say evenly, quietly.

Why does he have to stand so close? Your gaze shifts to his mouth, just for a moment. You hate that his lips pull into a smile. You hate that he is closing the gap between you, and you stand there like a wet duck.

He reaches down and quickly presses his lips against yours, gently at first, then more ardently. You feel yourself sinking into this familiar sensation, your body responding independent of your will. You give in to the frenzy, quickly slipping off the t-shirt and the wet bra, and soon, in a flurry of movements find yourselves on the daybed right there in the corner of his tiny living room. You hold on to him quelling all your misgivings when his lips close around one nipple and you force yourself to open your eyes. You look at the ceiling fan. It takes everything in you to speak.

"Stop," you say, so quietly you wonder if you have said it outside your head.

"Why?" He groans, but grudgingly rolls off you.

You sit up and pull the t-shirt over your nakedness. You look at him sitting with his back to you. He is still breathing raggedly.

"So, you and that man... together now?" he asks.

"That's not why I... I'm not with anyone," you say.

"But you been with someone else on this trip."

"I don't think that is any of your business anymore."

"I know you have," he says.

You remain silent for a moment. He looks back at you, his face unreadable, at first.

"And you had a whole child with your ex the minute things ended between you and me," you say. It is there, like always, hanging like a solid mass between you.

"We bringing up ancient history now?"

His laugh is hollow and harsh to your ears.

"She will always be in your life and I don't think I fit in it anymore. So what does it matter who I—"

"You wasn' even going to tell me you was back, right? If I never see you in the mall yesterday—"

"Why should I? We don't owe each other anything anymore. Remember?"

"So, it serious with this man?"

You look at him. His face more open with the pain of the thought.

You want to tell him it meant something it didn't, just to transmit a fraction of old agonies. *I did not plan it. He was someone from my high school days...but why does it matter?* He is someone you had thought about constantly as a teenager, someone rendered nondescript in the shadow of this decade-long affair with Warren. Funny how after a chance meeting with this old crush, how you found yourself at his apartment in Eltham Acres, a stone's throw from Warren's community, how easy and hollow and meaningless giving him your body was. You still do not know why you did it. You would struggle to explain it all to Warren.

He wasn't you, you want to say to Warren. *I don't know what I was doing there. I don't know what I am doing here.*

You watch Warren get up slowly and pull on his jeans.

"You want something to drink before you go?"

You ignore the hard edge in his voice.

"No. That's okay," you say. You get off the bed and stoop to grab your damp bra and panties from the floor. "Could you just...please bring my dress?"

He moves toward the fridge, then stops.

"You know... is you who broke it off with me first," he says.

"What?" you say, straightening. You try not to look at the hurt fresh in his eyes.

"Is because I am just some high school dropout, right? I wasn't good enough for you anymore."

You sigh.

"Everybody knows that long-distance...it just wouldn't work...plus, you didn't understand why grad school was important to me," you say. "We had other problems too...we were arguing all the damn time over everything, over nothing."

"It wasn't over nothing," he says, his voice low. "And I would-a waited for you, Marcy."

"Like you waited a whole month before fucking *her* and all the time you would call me crying how you missed me and have me feeling bad about breaking us?" you say.

"*You* left *me!*" He pulls on a merino hanging on the back of the chair. "I tired of saying the same thing over and over. You always the one leaving me anyway."

You pull on your underwear. You do not meet his eyes.

"You at least use protection with this man?"

You turn and look at him hard.

"Unlike you and *her* apparently," you say. "Now please go get my paintings and my dress."

"You have to wait until I wrap up the paintings," he says.

"You said they were ready."

"I said I took them off the wall, didn't I, Your Highness? Plus, you go need to get a taxi to bring all this. I won't be carrying them for you all that way."

You sigh. You watch him disappear into the room and then come out carrying two paintings in each hand. Then, he secures the frames together with masking tape, the glass encasing flush against each other for protection.

"Why didn't you just tell me yourself that you had a child? Why I had to find out on Facebook with everyone else?"

He stops taping.

"I knew it would just hurt you because..." he says.

You won't let him say it. You won't let yourself say it.

"It would have been better coming from your own mouth," you say.

You have tried to talk about this once before without success, devolving into angry standoffs and disconnected phone calls. One year stretched into two and you had resigned yourself to it until you saw the little girl so much like him in the flesh.

She had come with his ex-girlfriend unannounced at your last visit six months before. You had stood there, looking at how the child had his whole face already, her hair secured in two plaits and looping ribbons. You had not really looked at the woman, unable to take your eyes off the physical manifestation of all your fears. You had seen the girl-friend only in photos of the past before you, photos of the present after you, united through this little girl with ribbons and high cheekbones. You had stood there feeling superfluous, the air suddenly sucked out of the room. You had mumbled something about your flight back and slipped away. You had heard him call your name, but suddenly you were at the bottom of the lane on the edge of the main road before you could look back at the path, letting the strange mixture of regret and grief and confusion settle in your chest.

Warren straightens now, pulls on another shirt over his merino, and grabs the umbrella in the corner.

"Wait here. I need to get more tape," he says. Then, in two strides, he is out the door.

You get up and look down at one of the paintings of Coronation market you'd painted two months before graduate school.

"You always using too much paint. You don't need that much paint," he'd said that day. "Only this much you need."

He smeared a dime-sized dollop of yellow ochre on the bridge of your nose and you laughed. Then he spread out your limbs right there on your bedroom floor, peeled away the paint-splattered overalls and kissed you from crown to toes.

You waited as long as you could to do the inevitable, to hand him the envelope of your acceptance to that university in New Orleans.

He'd stood there shaking his head like you had told him you only had one month to live.

"I thought...I thought maybe you could come with me, maybe not right away...but eventually," you said.

"You knew what you were doing," he said.

He didn't speak to you for four days. And like a bad omen, when he put the market piece in the Mandeville Art Show, it did not sell. He told you the news, wished you well, and that was to be that.

He did appear in your apartment while your sister's car idled out front with the last of the suitcases at the very last moment.

"I always knew you was going to do big t'ings," he said.

You embraced. You blinked back tears. You promised to call every day. You said you would work everything out.

Then, at the end of your first year, someone congratulated him online about the birth of his baby girl and it felt like someone had thrust a shard of ice clear through your chest.

Now, Warren comes back into the room, a little wet despite the umbrella. You are sitting on the daybed still in his t-shirt cradling one of the paintings, one you'd painted of him.

"Why you giving me this one?" you say.

He brings the plastic shopping bag to the table and takes out a roll of tape.

"I figured I would give you back everything you ever did give me jus' like the first time you left me," he says.

He tapes another set of paintings together.

"I know you still blame me," you say in a small voice.

He continues to tape.

"I wanted that baby too..." you say, your voice cracking.

He stops taping. He takes a deep breath.

"I never did blame you," he says. "Not even when you say you didn't want to marry me anymore."

"It felt like you were angry with me when it happened..."

You try to keep your voice from shaking. You are failing miserably.

"But that is not how it was.... I wanted you no matter what," he says. "You the one decide that you had to get away from me... that you have to go all the way to America, right?"

"I just needed some time...some space to think..."

You know you have lost the battle with suppressing the tears. He moves to reach for you, but you move away.

Then, he fishes something from the shopping bag.

"How about a cease fire? I got your favorite," he says, branding a bottle of Rum Cream.

You shake your head. The last thing you need is to lose your wits, you think.

"You don't need to spend any money on me," you say.

"Is okay...I been selling work from my last show," he says. "You would know if you was still following me online."

You regard him for a moment. You wipe the corners of your eyes with the bottom of the t-shirt.

"I'm sorry...about everything," he says.

He puts down the bottle.

"Are you?"

"I don't know how to make it right, Marcy," he says. He stands there, his shoulders down. "What happen, happen...we cannot keep reliving it like this..."

You remember his face when you told him he was going to be a father, like some invisible force was pulling his lips upward with your every word. You didn't think about the fact that you had no money between you, that your parents and friends and church would denounce the whole thing. You lived in that moment of his acute and perfect joy.

And then the tiny fleshy mass violently expelled itself from your body months later and lay floating in a bloody pool at the base of the toilet bowl. You had stood in disbelief, feeling cold and desolate in the aftermath. You would not tell him the news for five days. Then, you could not abide his questions, each seemingly an accusation, a piercing. And even when he held you so close you could feel his heartbeat, you never felt more distant.

Perhaps he would have married you anyway, but you could not leave him with that burden.

You would decide for both of you.

You hate how dejected he looks now, just standing there.

"I'll take a sip of the Rum Cream," you find yourself saying.

He reaches for it again and pours some into two small glasses.

"I don't want us to be on bad terms, Marcy," he says, handing you a glass.

Then, you both sit there on the daybed silently sipping the Rum Cream for a while. You are not sure what else to say.

He picks up the small portrait you've been cradling. You look over at his hard jawline, the brown eyes penetrating you in that way he has, a lot of the unsaid swimming in them.

"You still paint?"

"Sometimes," you say. "But it... makes me think of you so..."

He shakes his head.

"You shouldn't let nobody stop you," he says. "Not even me."

"I know," you say. "It just doesn't make me happy anymore. I'll stick to my history books and other people's life stories for now."

You both let the silence hang there for a while.

"Maybe one day we will look back at all of this ...," you begin, but neither of you would believe that this could be revisited with humor at any point in the future. You swallow the rest with the last of the alcohol in your glass. You can feel the familiar mix of warmth and sadness course through you.

You look over at him. He holds your gaze for a moment.

"I think I go always love you no matter what you do, no matter what you say," he says.

"You think so?" you ask.

"I know so," he says.

You put the glass on the floor, take his and put it gingerly beside yours. Then you take his face in your hands. You look at him, your grief mirroring his. You kiss him. He remains still, only his lips moving against yours.

"Do you want to...?"

He stills when you do not respond.

You try not to look over at that image of him and his daughter. You try not to think how you would never share becoming first-time parents with him. You try not to think about a week before spent alone watching the Mardi Gras parades from your balcony on Chartres Street, feeling so lonely and thinking how Warren would have loved to stand next to you and sketch the outlandish costumed people walking by.

He pulls away, goes to the fridge, and reaches behind it for your dress.

"It's still a little damp but you can wear it now," he says, handing it to you.

You look down blankly at the floral print. A cry is climbing up your throat. You swallow hard.

"Thanks," you say. Your voice small and husky.

He comes and sits beside you once again.

"Listen," he says. "It not raining so hard now... I can help you carry the paintings if you like."

You look up at him, reach over, and slip your hands into his to feel the way he had held them as you both raced there through the rain.

"There's no rush," you say. "Maybe we can sit here until it stops."

"Yes," he says, looking down at where you are holding hands. "For the last time."

You do not miss the gloom in his voice or the way he rubs your fingers with his like he used to. His forehead touches yours. You listen to the drizzle punctuated by his breathing for a while. You move closer to him. He slips his hands from yours to put them around you, pulling you closer. He begins to rock you.

"Yes... the very last time," you murmur and close your eyes. Your mouth finds his. You do not notice when your dress slips from your lap onto the floor.

Limbo

Going to America

You know the tingling feeling you get when you are walking through a busy mall and you lock eyes with some stranger for a mini second. And that eye contact lingers in your head so that your heartbeat is racing faster than normal? That is me catching the tingling feeling and strutting my hips a little slower while running my hands through my box braids over and over again. The stranger is a he with fluttering eyelids and droopy eyes. His gaze follows me through the queue all the way to the counter where the sales attendant packs my groceries into a branded plastic bag. He is standing by the entrance when I come out of the mall, staring at me in a way that warms my skin. I let him take the shopping bags from me and he is saying that his name is Chiwetalu and he is not usually like this. I am walking a little behind him, soaking in his presence. He flags down a taxi for me to enter before asking for my number. Afterward, we go for lunch, dinner, movie, or whatever excuse we have so we can be together. I dump my current boyfriend when Chiwetalu gives me the spare keys to his apartment. I meet his parents, and when I introduce him to Momsy and my sister, they both confirm that he is the next best thing to happen to me after spaghetti and corned beef. As we are certain that Cupid sanctified our union, we tie the knot and live happily ever after. But I have digressed. So I will start from another beginning.

At the airport, my body is pressed against Chiwetalu's body and when we see that our three-month-old daughter Dian, is fast asleep and sucking her right thumb in the baby carrier, we probe into our tongues. His tongue tastes like the remnants of the *eba* and *egusi* soup he had for lunch. Mine tastes like smoked Titus fish. Only Titus fish because I am too happy and nervous to eat. Happy because he has finally gotten a six-month tourist visa that is going to make all our hopes and dreams come through. Happy because he will no longer work for that insurance firm that always owed in claims. Nervous because I don't know how long Dian and I will wait until he gets his papers and sends for us. Nervous because I've pondered incessantly on how he will navigate the weather, economy, and find stability.

I feel the glare of several pairs of eyes on us because our lips remain locked for longer than I can remember. Then he breaks it off and crosses the barrier. We try to maintain eye contact but can't since his back is turned away from me. I wave and he turns to wave until I cannot see his back anymore.

The butterflies circling in my stomach disappear one after the other. What remains is a sinking feeling of abandonment on the coaster bus ride back to the outskirts of the airport, followed by an anxiety I couldn't explain while breastfeeding Dian on the taxi ride back to our two-bedroom apartment. The cable remote sits where he left it on the glass centre table. I sit on the couch staring at the spot he would have occupied to watch television and cheer his football team. When Dian lets out a piercing cry, I run her a warm bath and I let her lie with me in the master bedroom where the sheets smell of his sweat and aftershave. I dream about all three of us, living in a house with a well-mowed lawn and backyard surrounded by rambling vines and climbing roses growing through an immaculately white picket fence. In the framed picture on the marble wall, his teeth are white, mine are whiter, and Dian is sprouting two front teeth.

After I count the hours and calculate the time difference twenty times over, his call finally comes through.

"How are you?"

"I am fine. You should see how Dian has been crying all afternoon, she knows you are gone."

"You sound as if I am dead."

"I miss you so much. You won't even understand."

"As soon as you finish your youth service, I will send for you."

"I know."

"What is it you are not telling me."

"I am just moody."

"Everything will be okay Ayo. I have to run. Kiss Dian for me."

"I love you."

"I love you too."

26

How it leaked to the neighbors that Chiwetalu traveled out last week still haunts me. We had kept the good news of his visa bound in secrecy, telling only a handful of relatives who were willing to help us raise travel funds. I remember now telling Moji, my friend, two days before he left. I assume that she may have spilled the news since she lives two streets away and frequents Bush Bar, the most popular gossip hub in our neighborhood. The news spread so much that even the neighbors who failed to acknowledge my existence before now, find it imperative to offer me congratulatory messages.

"Congratulations madam. I am happy for you people ooh."

"Thank you."

"I hope he is calling?"

"Yes," I reply with glee.

"When will you people join him?"

"Very soon."

I am beginning to worry that too many people know my husband now lives in Brooklyn with his cousin Chigor. The world being the way it is, you cannot tell who is happy for you and who has the ability to thwart that happiness. Combined with my midnight prayers and morning devotion, I beseech Momsy with prayer points to channel to the various angels and saints that she prays to. I cannot pray to those angels and saints on my own because my pastor says praying to dead people is tantamount to idolatry. Nevertheless, I ask her to pray to them, since prayers can never be too much.

The Mrs. Goes Job hunting

People think that I am immune to financial hardship because my husband lives in America. If only they knew that Dian and I have been living on my 25,000 naira monthly NYSC allowance for nearly five months before Chiwetalu called to say he had managed to land two jobs–helping out on construction sites during the day and cooking dishes in an African restaurant at night. He can only squeeze out $200 to send to me every month as he is saving to earn a master's degree. I in turn squeeze to save for house rent and our daily needs, preferring to shop for clothes and basic necessities for Dian and me at *katangwa* market rather than at any superstore or mall, and I unplug the cable for good. That money is hard to come by, does not stop me from paying my monthly tithes to my pastor so that God can hasten up in opening the windows of heaven to rain down his blessings on me. So that Chiwetalu can land a better paying job and settle quickly and send for us. Instead, he calls to complain about Chigor for the third time.

"Chigor has been acting funny these days, sending me on errands as if I am his mate. Leaving all the house chores for me to do. Locking me out of the apartment until he returns from work. Me that used to send him money for upkeep before he left for America. Ayo I have suffered."

"Sorry. Please just endure because of us."

"If not of papers I would have just gotten my own place since. So that all this nonsense can stop."

"I am praying for you. I am praying for us. All will be well."

I read on the internet that they are raiding neighborhoods around New York, looking for illegal migrants to send home. I call Chiwetalu repeatedly for four days and his number goes straight to voicemail. I panic on the fifth day and call Chigor. Chigor says Chiwetalu has moved out and did not leave a forwarding address, and adds something about how inappropriate it is for me to call him in the middle of his nap. I go on my knees and start to cast and bind any agent of darkness scheming to facilitate my husband's deportation. I tell them that they will not succeed neither will they bring me shame. After one agonizing month, the agents of darkness succumb and Chiwetalu calls.

"What happened?" I am inside *katangwa* market trying to find a quiet place to talk.

"I had to leave Chigor's place. I couldn't take it anymore."

"Where are you staying now?"

"I moved to New Jersey."

"Where?"

"Lambertville."

I am nodding to the phone as if I know where that is. "So who are you staying with there?"

"It doesn't matter who I am staying with. What matters is that I have left the house of that ungrateful bastard. His day of reckoning is coming."

I couldn't agree more.

It is starting to hurt now that Chiwetalu has stopped communicating on Skype and will hang up abruptly in between What's App video calls. The times are long gone when he recounts every detail of his day. Now, he is annoyingly tight-lipped and will not say what he is up to. I simmer in fury and decide to let him be because I am dealing with my own set of problems. The monthly NYSC allowance ended as soon as my batch passed out. I join the millions of Nigerian graduates looking for gainful employment. I fill out over thirty job applications from bank teller to business development officer to marketing positions. Many of the job descriptions do not list a B.Sc. in Environmental Biology as one of the prerequisites. I do not care, as it is better to spread my tentacles wide. I am not going to limit myself.

After waiting months for the recruiters to call me for interviews and none of them do, I drop off Dian at Momsy's place every morning and hit the streets. I leave my CV on the reception desks of all the companies along Acme Road and Oshodi-Apapa expressway. When the security guards won't let me go past the gate, I drop off my resume with them and squeeze 200 naira into their palms, clad with my most sheepish smile, before begging them to contact me whenever the company is re-cruiting. I still don't get any calls for interviews. I harass an uncle who knows another uncle who works in the Ministry of Youth and Women Development. He assures me that he will find me a spot if I call him again in three weeks. He has since stopped picking up my calls.

The text message says I have been shortlisted for an oral interview hold-ing at 9 am tomorrow in a Surulere address. The message does not say the name of the company or the job position, but I am elated that after the grueling months of submitting applications, I have finally made it to the interview stage.

I wear my only 'I am a responsible adult' ocean blue skirt suit and throw black cover shoes in my handbag to wear as soon as I enter the venue. I am shocked to see that the venue doesn't resemble anything of an office space. Several plastic chairs face a long table covered with a brown tablecloth I assume was once white. The dark-skinned girl with a ponytail sitting beside me asks if I know the name of the company and I say no. She says her name is Constance and she teaches social studies in an elementary school. She asks what I do for a living. I say I work freelance for a charity organization. My silver watch chimes 10:45 am and none of the interviewers have shown up. The room is getting rowdy and I am certain that the midday heat has cleaned off my foundation and eyeliner. A heavily built man in a black suit too tiny to have been his, stands in front of the long table and asks us to wait a little longer for his boss who is just returning from a very important breakfast meeting and is currently stuck in traffic. We wait and I drain my battery playing Candy Crush and stalking *Runtown* on Instagram.

The boss finally arrives at 12:50 pm after I down one bottle of Sprite with two sausage rolls that I purchased from a stall close to the venue. He does not apologize for coming late. Instead, he begins by saying, "The Holy Book says that my people perish, for lack of knowledge. It is information that keeps a poor man poor, and a rich man rich. I am here as an angel of light to make you rich."

I let out a semi-silent fart.

"How many of you have heard of the group Longevity?"

Two candidates raise their hands. He smiles and tells them that they are smart people on their way to success. The heavily built man in the ill-fitting suit passes around colorful flyers that show images of drug supplements and organic cleansers. The product descriptions claim to cure a variety of ailments.

"The market here in Lagos is massive and if you all can key in now as marketers, success will be your middle names." He cleans the sweat that gathers on his forehead with a white handkerchief. He goes on to tell us how he has built a four-bedroom flat in Lagos and is building a second house in his hometown from marketing and selling these products. Due to his commitment, he has earned a five-star position in the Longevity hierarchy and is able to go on vacations with his family annually to any destination of his choice.

"You can become like me in less than one year if you register now with only 20,000 naira." His voice is louder than when he first came in. When some of the candidates get up to leave, he calls them cowards who have just missed out on achieving greatness. However, we the brave ones still seated, can register with a discount and pay only 15,000 naira. My silver watch says 2:30 pm. I bid Constance farewell with a tap on her shoulder and the creaking sound of my cover shoes follow me out.

Cupid draws his bow

The itch comes to greet me often. Especially at that time of the month when the eggs descend accompanied by a whitish slippery discharge. I lie buried under my flowery print duvet, imagining that Chiwetalu is sending me to sixth heaven and back. Later I will superimpose him with Alex Ekubo melting into a 1990 version of Denzel Washington. Recently it is the face and body of Emmanuel, my neighbor who lives in the apartment complex beside mine and owns a cake and pastries store on Allen Avenue, that I imagine. In my itch-induced state, he is rubbing honey all over my stomach and is sucking on my belly button. In another stretch of fictitious time, it is a strawberry he places between my teeth. Before I can reward him for all his kindness, I have achieved an explosion of my own.

Last Sunday evening, Emmanuel came to my apartment with a stainless steel tray full of cupcakes. He set the tray down at the centre table, and after inquiring about Dian said, "So I am passing these cakes round because I want feedback on some flavors I recently invented for the 'switch flavors' event I am trying to organize."

"I am not sure I am the right person for this tasting fiesta." My mouth watered from inhaling so many flavors at once.

"*Haba* stop being modest. Take slices of each of them, then tell me what you think and I will write your comments down." He scribbled something I could not see on his notepad.

I chewed slowly, savoring the myriad of flavors seeping into my tastebuds while thinking of something grand to say. He stared at my mouth, I stared at his broad nose and thick lips. I said I loved the genuine coconut flavor in one of the cupcakes. He leaned forward and planted a kiss on my left brow and got up with a start to the door. With an agility I did not know I possessed, I got up quickly, pinned him against the door and let him eat all the cake in my mouth.

When Dian let out her usual piercing cry from her bedroom, I let him go and he left the entire contents of his tray on the centre table. He returned that night with a bottle of red wine and a packet of condoms.

A voluptuous brown-skinned girl with weave reaching her waist is standing in front of my door, asking if Emmanuel is in my apartment because she is unable to reach him on his mobile phone.

I say no then ask, "Why would you think he is here?"

"Because I heard he comes here frequently."

"No, he has been here just once." I realize that I am on the defensive and that my voice is shaky.

"Just so you know, I am his girlfriend."

"Congratulations." I bang the door against her face before she says anything else.

In less than an hour, Emmanuel sends me a text asking me to forgive the girlfriend episode. I do not reply. I stop picking up his calls and I stop imagining anything with him in it.

When Chiwetalu and I are on video calls, Dian touches the screen and calls him *Dada*. He smiles non-stop and reaches out to touch Dian's face on his screen. Today, as if on cue, his smile evaporates, and his face becomes sober like he is about to convey urgent news.

"There is something I have been meaning to say. I want you to hear it from me first."

My heartbeat skips.

"I had to marry a citizen."

"Blood of Jesus."

"It is a contract marriage. As soon as I get my green card, we will divorce."

"This is not our arrangement Chiwetalu. How could you even do it like this?"

"Do you know how many times they have raided my neighborhood to deport people like us without papers? I live in fear, I cannot even apply for good jobs. There is no other way. This is the only way." He is shouting into his screen.

"What is her name? Is she Black, white, Hispanic, or Asian?" I shout louder into my own screen.

"What does it matter?"

I hang up immediately and call Momsy to tell her. She says sorry and that my day of testimony will surely come. Because sorry isn't comforting enough, I call Temi to tell her too. She insists that kind of thing happens all the time. And I should join a closed Facebook group for women whose husbands are abroad just so I will know that I am not alone in the struggle. She sends me the link and I scroll through. I see that all the posts are stories of women who are stupendously happily married because their husbands live abroad. Or stories of husbands who come home to visit every Christmas, bringing more gifts than the wives could possibly accommodate. Or other stories of husbands who have sent letters of invitation to the embassy, so it is merely a question of months before the wives join them.

I leave the group in less than an hour. Apparently, I am alone in this struggle.

Chop and enjoy life

My friend Moji is sitting on the recliner on my porch, lamenting about how the entire universe is an unstable existence added to many of life's simultaneous equations that never really balance.

"What happened?" I ask.

"The Bush Bar is shutting down. Where will I buy nutritious pots of soup and stew during weekends? Or where will I step down with pepper soup and beer when I return from work?"

"And I thought this is about returning peace to South Sudan. Is that the only bar in this place?"

"How can you even ask this kind of question? That is the only place you can get *correct* pepper soup."

"Open your own bar and restaurant then."

"I cannot run a bar. I drink too much. And a restaurant is out of it because I cannot cook."

I start to chuckle when I recount the number of times Moji was too drunk to return home, and how her husband carried her home forbidding her from entering any bar again.

Once sober and fortified with salary payments, she returns to Bush Bar. "Even you can start the business and run it until your husband sends for you."

I say nothing, still fuming from the knowledge that my husband is married to someone else and I still do not know what to make out of what is left of my marriage to him.

"I don't know anything about running a bar," I say instead.

"Who told you there are separate skills for this type of business? You learn on the job."

Moji's suggestion plays crosswords in my head for several nights, and when I can no longer keep it to myself, I call Chiwetalu for the first time in weeks.

"Praise the Lord, you have finally remembered you have a husband."

"I want to open a bar."

"What do you know about running a bar?"

"That it is better than waiting for you."

"This master's I am studying for is costing me a fortune. I am not even able to save."

"How is your brand new wife?"

"I will send what I can tomorrow."

After he sends $300 dollars, I call Moji and she meets me at the empty spot where Bush Bar once stood. The landlady, a no-nonsense middle-aged woman in a loose fitting boubou gives me the keys when I pay her one year's rent. In the days that follow, I buy a variety of drinks and fry peppered chicken, snail sauce, and beef as starters. I put up a signpost in front that reads *Chop and enjoy life: Drinks, Pepper Soup and small chops available.* The customers trickle in.

When Moji brings other regular customers, I am finally able to reconcile the credit and the debit. I learn very quickly that the merrier the customers are, the more likely they are to keep drinking or to buy drinks for others. It is not unusual to have a customer order two or more crates of beer to be distributed to everyone at the bar because his wife has delivered a bouncing baby girl or boy or he has acquired a new car or girlfriend or has been promoted at work. This rakes in neat profits for me very quickly, such that I am able to purchase two loudspeakers and a flat-screen television for my customers to view live matches.

When people begin to demand food, I add rice and stew, eba and fufu with a variety of soups to the menu. It isn't long before the cooking and reheating overwhelms me and I put a *Cook and servers wanted* sign outside. Still, my bar would not be what it is without Jerry–the bulkier, bearded version of David Oyelowo who comes in every evening after work to order his usual dinner of rice and snail stew and says very little when he sits in his regular corner watching everyone. On many occasions, he helps me quell drunken brawls, and his demeanor keeps the randy customers at bay. Today he comes in earlier than usual and is swinging to the songs blasting from the loudspeakers.

"Is that Lighthouse Family?"

"Yep." I stare at his Adam's apple all the way to the knot of his tie and the white buttons on his striped blue and white checkered shirt.

"Which of their albums is that? I can't place the songs."

"It is a new studio album. Blue Sky In Your Head."

"So they are back after like what?"

"18 years." I chuckle.

He stretches out to link his arms with mine and we twirl around the bar.

Limbo

It is funny how the neighbors have stopped asking after Chiwetalu. They no longer want to know if he is calling or has found where to eat Nigerian dishes or still sends presents home. They are now more interested in knowing if I have found servers who are willing to stay or how they can connect me with their not-so-distant relation who will make an excellent cook. Then their attention shifts to Dian.

"Omo mi how are you?"

"*Ayam* fine," she replies.

"What did you learn in school today?"

Dian will attempt to recite the alphabets stopping at 'L' or 'M' or anywhere else memory serves her, before switching to nursery rhymes. They will applaud her for trying.

I am preparing tables in anticipation of the usual heavy Friday evening crowd when Temi calls in a tone so urgent that I ask her to calm down.

"Ayo you will not believe what I am seeing."

"What?"

"Search for Nicole Anyawu on Facebook."

I type the name and regret it immediately. Nicole's profile photo is a black and white close-up shot of her, Chiwetalu, and two young boys lying on their backs in a way that all four of them form a circle. They all appear interconnected and serene. I scroll down her page and see that her public posts oscillate between adverts for her pet food store and how fortunate she is to have Chiwetalu and their sons.

I draft a message to send to her.

I am Ayobami Anyawu. Chiwetalu and I are legally married and have lived as a couple for one brief but intensely passionate year.

Does he still keep the toilet seat lid open and leave a truckload of shit without flushing? Does he still talk in his sleep and wear soccer pants in place of boxers?

When I go to click send, a customer walks in and orders beef sauce to go with his beer. I clear the entire message when I realize my anger is directed at the wrong person. In a short while, the *TGIF* crowd fills the tables and my servers and I struggle to keep up with their demands.

It is only when I return home and put Dian to sleep that I call Chiwetalu.

"Who is Nicole Anyawu."

"My wife. Erhh I mean the person I told you I married so that I can secure my papers."

"Her Facebook profile says she has been married to you for four years. That means it was when you moved out of Chigor's house you married her."

"You do not understand how these things work."

"Have you not gotten your papers?"

"I have."

"So why are you still married to her?"

"It is just on paper."

"Those children on her cover photo and profile picture are they also for the papers? No wonder you have refused to send for me."

"Whatever you think Ayo, we are still very married and I still love you."

"You have said enough. Good night."

I hang up and call Jerry.

Upon learning about the success of my new business venture, my father-in-law and mother-in-law summon me to a meeting. I do not want to go alone so I arrive with Momsy and Temi. We sit in the living room and chew cabin biscuits with groundnuts, washing it down with canned malt drinks. After we run out of small talk, my father-in-law clears his throat dramatically.

"I hear you now run a restaurant and bar that attracts several men from within and outside Lagos."

"Women also come to my bar," I add.

"Is that a responsible thing for a respectable married woman to be doing?" He goes on as if he did not hear me.

"You are aware that your son is still married to a U.S. citizen who has two children for him?" Momsy says a little too loudly.

"Is he the first person to marry for papers?" my mother-in-law asks Momsy.

"That is no longer an issue for me. What worries me is that he has not seen me or his daughter in five years. Each year he keeps promising to come home or send for us and those are just empty promises."

I am trying not to sob.

"Only five years and you are complaining. What of those men that haven't returned after ten, twelve, or fifteen years? We know he is not in prison and he is hale and hearty and still sends you money. Does that not show his commitment?" My father-in-law is gesticulating with both hands and I start to see the man who rained infinite blessings upon me on my wedding day in new light.

To stop myself from crying, I head outside and Momsy follows me.

I stand still, thinking of a love I once had and swimming now in a limbo of uncertainty, wondering if the person who embodies that love will ever return.

Momsy is tired of standing still. She looks me in the eye. "Tell me now, are you still marrying that Chiwetalu? Let me know what to tell those people inside?"

"I don't know," I say, without returning her gaze.

The Tractor

There's a red tractor with a big, white bow on the bonnet in our yard. The grass underneath the tires could pass for a tufted carpet, and I've arrived in time to witness my mother, Mayo, snipping the bow with hedge shears. She laughs when Tata's clumsy ascent ends with him plopping into the tractor seat, her guffaw drowning out his soft chuckle as usual.

"It has suspension," Tata says, bouncing up and down, wiggling from side to side as if testing a new mattress.

His smile disappears behind his fat salt-and-pepper moustache when he sees me marching up the sun-baked driveway. I ignore his pleading eyes and stop in front of Mayo. Close enough to inhale the sweat with a hint of cocoa butter lotion emanating from her navy blue overalls.

"Another gift and you let him take her?" I say, shaking my head.

Mayo holds my gaze. "Your sister chose to return to her matrimonial home with her husband."

Matrimonial home. Husband. Jibes to remind me I'm still single at twenty-six. I chew my lip, tasting the vanilla flavored lipstick I had re-applied before coming home from work—even though the school is just down the road. The begrudging stares from my former teachers turned colleagues when I strut into the staffroom with my made-up face and colorful A-line dresses is worthwhile.

A triumphant flicker dances in Mayo's eyes, but her deflecting tactics are futile. The issue remains: my sister Kaweme's frequent, sometimes prolonged visits, and her husband, Greyson, guilt-tripping her into going back.

First, Greyson hired two workers to help Mayo and Tata around the farm. Then he bought them a generator. And now the tractor. Each gift more generous than the last, conveniently proffered when Kaweme deserts their home.

"Did you ask him why she keeps leaving?" I ask.

Out of the corner of my eye, I see Tata folding his arms over his paunch. The late afternoon sun bounces off his bald head.

Mayo shifts her attention to the aloe vera and roses growing around the foundation of the house. Her prickly babies. I swear they get more affection from her than I ever will.

"The first year of marriage is the hardest. Greyson and Kaweme will adjust," she says.

I know there are conversations I'm not privy to because I'm not married.

Never share your problems with singles. I've seen married women caution each other on Facebook, and noticed how some conversations end abruptly when I walk in on the female teachers chatting in the staff toilet. To uphold this custom of secrecy, the elderly women Mayo had organized for Kaweme's *Amafunde* wouldn't let me sit in during the traditional premarital lessons. I know single women who claim to have passed through these teachings as silent observers, taking mental notes on how to care for and please a husband in and out of the bedroom. But these gatekeepers shooed me away like a girl, denied me entry into my sister's room, even though she is four years younger.

"*Inshita yobe ikesa,*" they said. Your time will come.

Drums pulsated on the other side of the door. Singing poured out whenever someone stepped out to answer their phone or to dash to the toilet. I started returning home after the women had left. Sometimes, I'd find Kaweme untying a wrapper from her waist, folding it carefully as if the golden nuggets of wisdom bestowed upon her clung to the fabric.

I should leave my parents to revere their gift. Go inside, ease into my Friday evening with some Amarula and YouTube. But the Leo in me won't allow it. I'm compelled to investigate for cracks.

"But how will they adjust if Kaweme—"

"Natasha!" Tata growls at me.

Even the free-range chickens scratching at the ground behind the tractor jump.

Every so often, Tata shocks us by seizing power from Mayo, who is the mouthpiece for their marriage. When our bickering gets out of control, Tata screams at Mayo and me to stop until his body trembles and spittle flies from his mouth. Afterward, he retreats into the garage, tinkers with the battered Nissan Sentra, and ignores us for days. Not even the smell of fried, fresh bream can lure him to Mayo's kitchen for a bite before mealtime. And Mayo and I walk on eggshells around each other till the balance is restored.

Now Tata warns me through clenched teeth, making the dimple in his chin more pronounced, "This isn't your classroom. *Umuchinshi.*" Respect.

I don't need a mirror to tell me the little depression in my own chin is visible too. Or that my bulb-like nose also swells when I'm annoyed. My resemblance to my father started my obsession with makeup. When puberty hit, I learned to accentuate my femininity with eyeliner and padded bras. I'd sneak into my parents' bedroom to steal Mayo's waist beads and repurpose them into earrings, chokers, and bracelets. Anything to stop people referring to me as Tata's duplicate while calling my sister the *pretty one.*

True to her name, Kaweme is a natural-born beauty with facial features I can only attain through heavy contouring. Slim face, elegant eyebrows, pert nose. Blessed with Mayo's honey-brown skin, and legs fit for the runway. And yet she doesn't even own a pair of heels.

Tata points to something in the tractor, and Mayo moves closer, feigning interest, so she doesn't have to deal with me. I hoist my laptop bag over my shoulder and proceed into the house.

At the doorway, I stumble over Kaweme's slippers. Another excuse for her to come over. Two months into her marriage, she came back for an old sweatshirt and ended up staying the night. About a week for a book. And longer than that to drop off some chicken feed.

On my way to my room, I pause outside Kaweme's. The door is wide open. The curtains are looped through the burglar bars; the light falls onto the double bed with mismatched bedding. Bare walls, no rugs or throws. Just bland.

Mayo's laughter spews in through the window. I wander across the room to peep what they are up to.

She is talking on her phone and playing with the big white bow, flying it like a kite. "Have you seen the pictures I sent Pa WhatsApp? Yes...Yes. Kaweme's husband bought it for us. I tell you, he is such a blessing."

This is what Mayo always wished for. A fully functioning commercial farm with the equipment and labor to generate income like our neighbors, whose produce are stocked in supermarkets. Once, I'd overheard Mayo telling a relative she wasn't a farmer's wife, that Tata was just a man whose mother had bequeathed him six acres of farmland.

Meanwhile, Tata is circling the tractor, stroking the fenders, standing back to admire it. The tractor gleams, as if soaking it all in.

***

If I hadn't shown Greyson a picture of the tractor, it wouldn't be here.

That day, he'd showed up with a bottle of Moet and a box of Belgian chocolate truffles. He and Kaweme had been seeing each other less than a month and the unannounced visits were evidence of how smitten he was. Mayo ushered him into the sitting room and zoomed off to get my sister. Greyson sat on the floral-patterned armchair, which clashed with his cobalt blue suit and tan Oxfords. From the sofa across the room, I watched him twiddle with his cufflinks, shuffle the champagne and truffles around on the coffee table.

In a pitiful attempt to catch his attention, I picked up the *Zambian Farmers monthly* and pointed to the cover.

"If I had the money, I'd buy this for my parents."

Greyson got up and leaned over the sofa to see what I was talking about. When one end of his scarf brushed against my thigh for a second, the realization that our touching would never exceed shaking hands squeezed my heart.

Kaweme had come in then, and he lost interest in the picture. Same way he'd lost interest in me after he'd slowed down to ask for directions to a nearby farm, and Kaweme had popped out of nowhere, intruding on the moment. Greyson had met me first but fallen for her.

***

The first time Kaweme wore makeup, she was seventeen. She woke up one morning and told me she wanted to compete for the crown of Miss Lusaka High, a month before the event. Those days, I was adamant about becoming a makeup artist, but living in Makeni, a farm area, means taking two bus rides to the suburbs.

I'd walk to the thatched *kantemba* down the road, and chat with the cross-eyed man selling sweets and mobile scratch cards while waiting for a bus to town. Most times, I was late for appointments because no matter how hard I rapped the casing of my cosmetic wheelie bag, bus drivers and their conductors wouldn't leave until half the seats were full.

It excited me when Kaweme asked me to help her prepare for the pageant. It had been four years since I had completed high school myself, I was hoping something positive would come out of this. Two of the judges were popular models, and newspaper journalists would be present. Kaweme's win would be mine as well. I imagined the satin sash with the words *Miss Lusaka High* printed in a lovely cursive font across her chest, and a tiara atop her natural puff. In her *Times of Zambia* interview, she'd thank me for her makeup and wardrobe. Especially for her traditional costume, a dress I'd made from a white woven sack and embellished with red, black, green, and orange beads—colors of the national flag. Had I known she'd mess up, I wouldn't have wasted my time.

On the day, Kaweme walked on stage and missed a step, forgot to pose, and suppressed giggles at her mistakes. I should have known it was too good to be true. Adolescence hadn't transformed my sister the way it had transformed me. She still sat in trees eating ripe mangoes with her best friend Anna, who spent more time at our house to escape the flock of nieces and nephews roaming their farm. Kaweme still got up at daybreak and spent the entire day in dusty gumboots; planting, weeding, and harvesting. Trips to town didn't excite her. Without a doubt, the perfect heir to our parents' estate.

I didn't say a word on the drive home. Judging by how Mayo was flying through portholes and grinding gears, she was just as unimpressed with Kaweme's performance. If Anna wasn't in the car with us, Kaweme would have sensed the brewing tension. Instead, she was laughing and kneeing into my seat at her friend's dramatic stories about sharing a bedroom with four little nieces.

After we clambered out of the car, Kaweme trudged to unload the garment bags and shoes from the boot, but I nudged her aside with my elbow. She exchanged a furtive glance with Anna and turned to escort her home. But Mayo blocked Kaweme's path and declared, "This foolishness ends now!"

I lifted the bags inside, shuffled past Tata as he scurried to inspect his car. In my room, I grabbed the scissors and cut the costumes. If I didn't have Tata's manly torso, I'd have kept them for myself. Not long after, I swallowed my pride and enrolled at Punzisani Teachers Training College.

***

It's Sunday morning. As I had predicted, Kaweme is here to collect her house slippers. The silver Pajero drives into the yard minutes after Mayo and Tata leave for church. I don't blame her; I had waited till they took off before emerging from my room myself.

Mayo has funny ways of chasing Kaweme back to her home. She'll put a bag of tomatoes and spring onion in Kaweme's arms and say, "I picked these for you." Or she'll find Kaweme pouring herself a cup of *munkoyo* and say, "Don't finish that. Would you like me coming to your house and drinking your husband's favorite drink?"

It's amusing because, with me, Mayo doesn't skirt around anything. Those soft gloves came off the instant she heard I had lost my virginity.

"You're doing grown woman things so I'll talk to you like a woman."

But I wasn't a woman. I was a fifteen-year-old girl who'd made the mistake of sleeping with a boy who bragged about it to his friend. When his friend asked me if it was true, I slept with him to show the first boy he was nothing special. Hurt for hurt. But it backfired. Those boys told everybody at school. A teacher got wind of it and shared it in the staffroom. No one noticed the cleaning lady with her ears perked up in the corner. She also worked as a casual farm laborer, and later that day, she'd be plucking and dressing chickens at our farm.

Since then, Mayo and Tata treat me like bruised fruit; they know there's some good in me, but the marks are hard to overlook.

I'm in a lightweight bathrobe and headscarf, standing by the kettle when Kaweme strolls into the kitchen.

"Hey," she says. "I forgot my slippers."

"Mhm."

Whatever is going on with her is none of my business. If she's suffering from homesickness, it's her fault. Why marry a city boy if you love the feel of wet soil in between your toes?

Her phone is vibrating in her jeans, but she pulls a kitchen towel off the oven handle and starts drying the dishes. She does this all the time, says she's here for something and then slips right back into her old routine. Cleaning, refilling the feeders, and replacing the lightbulb heaters in the chicken run.

Nine months married, and the only change is her appearance. She's wearing a white halter top, and her pixie cut wig reminds me of 2010 Rihanna. I wonder if she and Greyson reminisce about the first time they met and laugh about the discolored t-shirt she was wearing over her leggings.

I was wearing a lilac dress, I had flat ironed my wig, and my makeup was flawless. Mayo stopped pushing a wheelbarrow full of manure to shake her head at me when I bustled past on my way to work.

"All this dress up for what?"

As I sauntered down the dirt road, a silver Pajero slowed down beside me.

The window rolled down to reveal a handsome thirty-something-year-old man.

"Excuse me, I'm looking for Bowa Farms?" he said.

I pointed behind us. "That one, in the barbed wire fence."

He peered over his shoulder and said something about an ad in the newspaper, and land for sale. I half-listened. I was gawking at the groomed beard around his firm jaw and wondering if his soft looking lips were blacker than his face because of smoking. The woody scent drifting from his car told me he liked rich perfumes that plant you in people's minds without them realizing. Only for them to remember you each time they sniffed it somewhere else.

That's when Kaweme appeared, waving my phone in my face. "You forgot this on the kitchen table."

I wanted to shove her into the bush for interrupting us. When I turned back to him, I knew I had lost him before I even had him. The way his eyebrows and shoulders shot up when he looked at her, how he quickly introduced himself and said, "This kind lady was just giving me directions to Bowa Farms."

Kind lady. My face sagged like it had a leak.

When Mayo tells her church friends about how Greyson and Kaweme met, you'd think she was there in the flesh. In her version, I'm an extra in the background. Her favorite part is that Greyson is the oldest son of a prominent politician. I'd watch her serve him and my sister hot chunks of pumpkin and send him off with bags of fresh maize and vegetables. Three months later, I had to walk out amid a lesson on adjectives because my phone wouldn't stop flashing on my table. Mayo stuttered, "Your sister, engaged," into my ear. All I could say was *Beautiful* over and over as I stared at the piece of chalk in my damp palm.

Kaweme's phone won't stop buzzing. Whoever is calling is relentless. She sighs and yanks it out of her front pocket.

I pour hot water into my mug and watch the red teabag bleed. Revisiting certain memories is like peeling the scab off a wound.

"Will you be long in the bathroom?" Kaweme asks.

"Why? You need something?"

She nods, then shakes her head, distracted by her phone. "No, I can take my things from the cupboards when you're done."

"Do it now. I might be long. Some of us have to scrub hard just to look half as beautiful."

Kaweme stares at me with astonishment. I regret my words immediately. All our lives, I have never acknowledged her good looks to her face. Now that I have, it's as though I've admitted my unattractiveness to us both. I feel like cowering behind the rickety saucer cabinet in the corner.

To save face, I put her under the spotlight. "Mayo and Tata are grateful for the tractor."

She turns her back on me to hang the tea towel. "You know what Greyson is like."

"No, I don't. What is he like?" I sip my tea. It needs more honey. "Does he beat you? Treat you bad? Is that why you're here all the time?"

Kaweme spins to face me. "What? What are you talking about? Greyson is not that kind of man."

"Then what's the problem? He worships you, gives you money, lets you drive his cars."

I follow Kaweme's eyes to the mess I've made. There's honey all over my mug and on the counter. I had forgotten the squeezy bottle was still in my hand.

"We have nothing in common," she says, and exhales like she's relieved.

"Then why did you marry him so fast? I doubt you even knew his middle name when Tata walked you down the aisle!"

I brush past her as I reach for the damp wipe cloth.

Kaweme folds her arms. "What about you? Did you ask those boys you slept with their middle names?"

Right in the gut. I try to think of a clever comeback but draw a blank. The condescending tone when she said 'those boys' reminds me of Mayo asking why I was opening my legs to everybody.

I tried to correct her, told her two boys weren't everybody, but Mayo wouldn't listen. She raised her voice, so I raised mine.

Tata silenced us both by slapping his palm against his thigh. "These are matters a father shouldn't know about his daughter!" His face contorted in what I translated as disappointment.

When I knelt at his feet, Tata refused to look at me. He stomped off to the garage. He didn't speak to me for weeks.

If Mayo had pulled me aside and not shamed me in front of my father, Tata would still love me. He'd still call me *my daughter*, like it's a pet name.

Our first fight as women and Kaweme takes the crown. She leaves me in stunned silence, with sticky hands.

When I was little, Tata used to grin at me when Mayo complained about my hard-headedness.

"Maybe she'll grow up to be a lawyer," he'd say.

I could have been a lawyer. But when people started calling me the *village bicycle*—a reputation I could never shake off no matter how hard I tried—I lost direction. My grades dropped, my teachers looked at me with judgment, my friends forsook me because their mothers told them to. I have never felt so seen and yet so alone as I did those days. Though it took a lot of effort to walk with my head high and my back straight, I did it. My tears and sadness were a well-kept secret between my pillow and I.

Look at her, she has no shame, everyone said. Everyone, including my own mother.

***

I'm not sure how long I've been pacing and biting my nails. I'm repulsed at the thought of nail varnish and tiny bits of skin in my stomach, but I can't seem to stop. The soft bristles on the makeup brushes that sit in a vase on my dresser appear to have lost their soothing effect. Normally, caressing them calms my nerves. Perhaps a warm bath will do the trick, except I can't get myself to leave my room.

I rub my knuckles together and pad around the carpet at the foot of the bed. Knowing that Kaweme is in the next room infuriates me. I want to knock down the wall separating us and put her in her place. The audacity to dredge up something I did a decade ago and sling it in my face. At least I have a life, and I have tried to venture away from this place. Apart from marrying Greyson, what interesting thing has she done? Even that is proving too high a task for her simple mind. And yet she mocks my past?

Why won't people let me forget?

On the first day of college, the prospect of a fresh start excited me. I sat at the front of the class, laid out my new pens and multi-colored Post-it notes. Then someone I went to high school with walked in and sat behind me. Whenever there was laughter and whispering in the back, I suspected it was about me. I imagined fingers pointing at me as the rumor snaked from row to row; the venom spreading fast, poisoning everyone against me. By the time I graduated, I had made two friends.

No one knows I haven't been with anyone else apart from those two boys, who moved on, untainted. Sometimes I wonder what would have happened between Greyson and me if Kaweme hadn't brought me my phone. It's the unanswered question, a weight on my mind each time I see him. Thinking about it now boils my blood. I can't let Kaweme win this fight. She already has Greyson's love, and Mayo and Tata's favor. The least I can do for myself is win this argument. I tramp to her room and barge in. She's not here.

I check the bathroom and every room in the house. No luck. I charge outside, the car is still here, next to the tractor. I even peek in the garage. Without the Sentra, this space is just a void.

The only other place I can think of is the chicken run. Pebbles prick my bare feet as I tread the winding footpath behind the house. The smell of chicken feed and poop gets stronger as I approach the weathered brick building.

It seems she isn't here either. The door is shut. There aren't other noises aside from the clucking and fluttering of wings. I almost turn back, then I hear laughter and mumbling. I crack the door, peep inside, and see Kaweme and Anna. Their foreheads are pressed together, their arms around each other's waists. I realize I have stumbled upon something private and intimate when Kaweme spots me and her right hand flies to her mouth, the left pushing Anna away.

Anna staggers backward and swings around to discover my puzzled face. She shrinks, her chest caves in, as though awaiting severe reprimand.

My eyes shift to Kaweme, who, like me, seems frozen in place.

The arsenal of words I had lined up before has disappeared.

Car doors thudding shut echo in the distance. Mayo and Tata are back from church.

"Please don't tell Mayo, she won't forgive me this time," Kaweme says, half bending her knees.

"Mayo knows?" I ask.

Anna studies my face. "Natasha won't tell. You guys are sisters. Sisters keep each other's secrets."

That might be true for her and her six sisters, not for us. When Kaweme discovered I had my nose pierced after I turned seventeen, she told Mayo. Not long after, I saw Kaweme give Anna a black plastic bag, which Anna carried carefully before disappearing into the maize field. I knew it contained eggs. For months, our parents had been complaining about how the chickens were laying less than usual, so I tipped Tata.

"Mayo knows?" I ask again, this time entering into the wire partitioned room.

"Natasha please. Mayo has given me so many chances-"

I stop her with a raised palm. "When did she find out?"

Kaweme stares at her suede ankle boots. "Before Miss Lusaka High. She forced me to do it, said if I spent more time doing girly things, I'd have no time to engage in foolishness. She calls it foolishness." Her trembling voice trails off.

I clasp my hands under my chin.

"We tried to be discreet, but she found us several times. Last time, Mayo made me swear while holding her bible to never let the devil use me again or she'd tell Tata. You know how unforgiving they are. Now imagine what it would be like for me...with another woman."

Now I understand why I saw Anna less and less after the Miss Lusaka High fiasco. And why Kaweme had chosen another friend as her bridesmaid. It made sense too, seeing as Anna had to step up and help her mother raise the grandchildren her sisters dumped on their mother. Nowadays I only see Anna at the school gate, combing one niece's hair while yelling at the other for having one sock on, and then threatening to whip the nephews if they don't go straight home after school. It never occurred to me Mayo didn't want her around for reasons other than her frivolity. Even the t-shirt Anna is wearing now has a cartoon of a curvy, Black girl mooning. It seems Mayo read the signs; the way Kaweme loosened up around Anna, the way they looked at each other and grinned like they had a secret language.

I glance at the chickens pecking in the wire enclosure. "What about Greyson?"

Anna lets out a scoff and Kaweme gives her chastising glare.

"Mayo was breathing down my neck, I had to act quick. Greyson came along at the right time. You said it yourself, he worships me, he'll do anything for me...for our family."

"Kaweme, you can't do this to him. It's evil and selfish," I say.

When Anna nods in agreement, Kaweme reminds her where the money she used to pay for her nephew's tonsillectomy came from. Anna tries to explain she didn't agree with the evil part, just that it's wrong to lead Greyson on. I walk out, leaving them to their tiff.

"Natasha please," Kaweme trots after me with Anna in tow.

"Can't you see I didn't have a choice?"

I hurry toward the house, unmoved by her pleading. Not having a choice is working at the school you attended all your life because none of the thirty-four application letters you sent out yielded fruit, and staying with your parents because your salary can't afford you the lifestyle you deserve.

We find Mayo and Tata standing in front of the tractor. Mayo stops listening to Tata, who is directing her attention to the field before them. She squints at Kaweme. "Your husband called. Why aren't you picking his calls?"

"You know why," I say.

Mayo's face droops. She knows I know. She knows I have the ammunition to destroy our lives.

"What's going on?" Tata asks.

No one says anything. Kaweme sniffles, and Anna puts her arm around her. I laugh because Mayo flinches at the gesture. They all look at me like I'm mad. They don't understand how I feel. The daughter who redeemed the family is just as flawed as I am. I want to rejoice and pound my fists into the ground. Except, our mother guards Kaweme's secret and shields her in a way I can't grasp.

I refuse to regard Kaweme as a victim. She is Mayo's accomplice. Though Mayo is using her as a pawn to milk Greyson, Kaweme is using Greyson to conceal her true self, and she is using his wealth to pacify our mother. I dab my eyes with my sleeve before the tears fall.

Tata takes off his checked flat cap and holds out his hand. "Come, my daughter. Walk with me," he says.

Mayo is begging me with her eyes. Beads of sweat sit on her top lip. She unbuttons her blouse.

I link my fingers with my father's and let him lead the way. It's like discovering an old glove and it still fits nice and snug. I'm broken and whole all at once. We walk down the driveway to the sing-song of a lone bird on a stunted tree to our left. Where are the others? Did they abandon it? By the look of it, the bird has a lot to say.

"I always wanted to be a mechanic," Tata says after a while.

"Why didn't you go for it? What happened?" I ask.

He places his hat on my head.

"Most times in life, we are stuck between what we want and what is right, especially when family is involved...I will tell you all about it someday."

I look over my shoulder to see Kaweme and Anna walking in the opposite direction. Mayo drapes her body over the bonnet of the tractor, her shoulders heaving up and down.

"We have time, tell me now, Tata."

Phantom Itch

It was Zulfaa's destiny to be seen and not heard. The problem with sight was that it was hind and fore, and its most recent update included an x-ray feature. And silence wasn't ever empty. Maybe silence in Mbalala gana, her village in Northern Nigeria, could pass for void—because the people there begged it to be—but not in Chicago. Silence in Chicago was unsettling and the unsettled filled it with meaning till it was empty no more. Zulfaa had only to offer some nothingness and Americans would see mystery.

And everyone knows that mystery+Americans=adventure!

American moms took one look at Zulfaa's pursed lips and floor-length skirts on the subway and saw regalness and grooming, chastity that was out of their reach, and a quiet piety that they would never know. They begged her with their eyebags and polite smiles featuring quivering jaws (a souvenir from their sleep deprivation), to bestow a smile upon their perusing infants as one would ask blessings of the Pope or the Dalai Lama, who was more popular these days. Their men saw her veiled head and thought, "Aaah, Nubian Princess"; they masked their sighs as cold shivers, accepting that this one fantasy was doomed to non-fruition.

X-RAY

I masked my cold shiver as a sigh of relief as I set Zulfaa's frame back upright. "Are you all right?" I asked. The tram had lurched forward, and I grabbed Zulfaa just in time to stop her from falling teeth-first onto the safety pole. Her eyes were electric and as I looked into them, they felt familiar; I knew that electricity because my own body still tingled with it—adrenaline from moments ago.

Saving Zulfaa was rather convenient, it gave me an opening. I had spotted Zulfaa's persimmon-colored hijab as I got on the tram and I was utterly shocked. The shade was so flamboyant that it hurt my eyes. On a train full of commuters at the end of a work day at the peak of winter, Zulfaa's hijab was the only non-gray thing in sight. And in response, it seemed, to her rebellion of outlandish color, the other bodies on the train had unanimously agreed, wordless, that she deserved her own island amid the sea of human sardines.

When she looked up and I saw her face, I was immediately glad that the only available spot was right beside her.

I reveled in my current glory as Hero: savior of Zulfaa, ready to claim my prize. What does a hero do though, with a mystery of a damsel? The heroes from the epics I had read as a boy had raging wars to turn to as they put off facing the women for whom they plunged into battle. I couldn't possibly fight the tram now, could I? So, there I was, a hero in distress.

Zulfaa came to my rescue by shrugging her shoulders so that my hands slid down her arms. *Arms!* I thought. I had momentarily forgotten that I still held on to her shoulders. I immediately reprimanded myself for interfering with the pristineness of her. *Arms*, the reminder that Zulfaa had a body; she wasn't just a floating face anchored by layers and layers of fabric.

Bodies, curious things that have crevices that hold (the answer to) riddles such as: What would make your nipple shudder, my lips or my tongue? If I trail the length of your spine with essential oils on my fingertips, will the weight of your buttocks fill my palms in reward at the end of the trail? We invented clothes that our imaginations, teased, may soar unhinged from the restraints of the perceptible.

Having successfully demonstrated my saving capabilities, Zulfaa took me home with her that night. The streets were dangerous and "Having a strong man like you with me would make me feel safe," she said. I saw Zulfaa home safely, but I didn't go my way because, "It is really cold and I couldn't possibly send you on your way without a cup of tea at the very least," she said.

Zulfaa's cup of tea warmed my hands, burned my tongue and clawed the back of my throat like sand. The tea was wrong the way a dry-eyed new widow is wrong and a drunk in anguish is wrong. One did not end up in a hijabi's room drinking her tea. To do so would be a crime against imagination and fantasy, the only realms where hijabis frolic with men of the West, like me.

After tea, Zulfaa and I had sex. How it happened was, Zulfaa took my teacup of from my hands and said, "You made it here, you might as well claim your prize." With that, she took my hands in hers and placed a condom in them. "You be safe now, I'm African," she taunted. Inside Zulfaa, I found confusion. I felt ridges where I knew there weren't supposed to be any. Surprise hills pressed against my genitals and led me down hollowed expanses that felt like there was no end in sight. Zulfaa laughed at the confusion on my face and enfolded me in her grip, thrusting me even deeper into herself. I prided myself on being familiar with the female anatomy and yet Zulufaa's insides were like nothing I had ever known.

When it was finished, Zulfaa sat smoking a cigarette on the bed. "The problem with men who have big penises is that you think that having a big penis absolves you of the work that your smaller-sized brothers latch onto as an opportunity to validate their manliness."

I lay in silence on the bed, confounded. The person before me was nothing like the desperately vulnerable naïf whose sanctity had been too strong for me to resist that I followed her home on our first encounter. Her now apparent worldliness seemed like the antithesis of the woman whose face crumpled in anguish as she bit down on her metal bed frame to force back the screams I could hear regardless in her throat, mounting with each thrust of my hip.

"It's wrong, it's all wrong, you, this...what have you done to me? Who are you? What are you and why are there ridges in your vagina?"

I wheezed as my panic began to rise.

She put out her cigarette on her desk and said, "Chill, you're not going to end up in a history book as the man whose lust plunged him into an alien's vagina. It's just simple old Female Genital Mutilation that's all. I take it that you've never stuck your penis in a mutilated woman, one with nothingness and keloids in place of a clitoris."

HIND

Zulfaa loved Chicago winters because they reminded her of home. Home, however, in terms of meteorology, was nothing like here. Home was the savannah, and it goes without saying that it was as hot as it was dry. Except in harmattan when it was all the aforementioned yet windy with no mercy and bitterly cold in the mornings. The harmattan winds came from the Sahara with more dust than you realized was contained in the world. Try as her mother did, there was no stopping Zulu from standing in the path of the wind to receive her daily coating of dust. Zulfaa particularly liked the way the dust settled on her lashes so that it fell to her cheeks when she batted her eyelids. Her skin was the same shade as the dust—mahogany with rich red undertones—so that long before there were makeup brands with forty foundation shades, Zulu had solved the Black woman's unique struggle of finding makeup that matched her skin tone. This was important because Zulu's mother forbade her from wearing makeup.

That was one decision Zulfaa could not understand. Her mother was hailed as Hauwa the Beautiful. She watched as her sisters were adorned with beads in their hair, waist beads, and Kajal under their eyes. When she walked with them, she stepped to the rhythm of the music of their waists because her own steps were silent. Her mother seemed to have enough appreciation for vanity until it concerned her.

One after the other, men trooped to her father's house to state their intentions toward her older sisters—her mother was the last wife, married in her father's old age. Zulfaa dreamed of the day when men would come for her, which was why she was confused when her mother introduced a morning routine of binding her chest in rolls of tightly knotted fabric as soon as she turned eleven and her breasts began to show.

Chest-binding wasn't the only thing her mother did to tuck away her budding femininity. Zulfaa wore her sisters' hand-me-downs just like every other girl did, but unlike everyone else, she wore her hand-me-downs several sizes too big because her mother would not let her get them shaped and slim-fitted. Hauwa also launched a personal vendetta against any man who as much as gave her daughter a second glance until everyone knew to steer clear.

Her efforts were enough until Zulfaa turned fourteen and Boko Haram came.

Each day, word reached them of a new village that had fallen to Boko Haram and how the village girls, once kidnapped or raped, usually both, became unrelenting groupies. Girls whose parents had previously been defiant enough to send them to school were hurriedly taken out. Still, Hauwa marched her daughter to school every morning until the sneers became too loud to ignore: "Does Hauwa think that her daughter is too good to be married off just like her peers? She has to be a bad mother else, why deny her daughter the security of a husband's covering more so at this time of grave insecurity?"

At long last, Zulfaa's mother decided that her best course of action would be to send Zulfaa away to boarding school in the neighboring village, Chibok. Amongst other reasons, the fact that this was an all girls school made no small contribution to Hauwa's decision. But first, she was going to ready her daughter by all means necessary. She readied her new school uniforms and food provisions and doled out cautionary tales daily. One evening, after Zulfaa had secured a place at the school, Hauwa led her at dusk to the very edge of the town, they were going to visit an old friend she said. As they walked deeper and deeper into the thicket, Zulfaa couldn't help but wonder if her mother's friend had a communicable disease or had committed such grave haram as to be ostracized from the rest of society. When they finally arrived at a crumbling hut in the middle of nowhere, Hauwa led her daughter into the hut and into the arms of two women waiting in the glow of a smoking kerosene lantern.

"Welcome Zulfaa, you are here to become a real woman," was all the warning she got before they pinned her to the ground and spread her legs apart. Her mother sat softly on her belly and spread her arms out crucifixion style as the second woman wielding a sickle began to harvest Zulfaa's clitoris. If Zulfaa had not been drowning in terror at that moment, she would have learned what an orgasm felt like for only an instant as her clitoris lay between the woman's fingers just as she began to carve new paths inside Zulfaa's genitals. Such was Zulfaa's deliverance from Stockholm Syndrome; for thus forth, even if she was kidnapped and/or raped, her will would not succumb to the sick sweetness of a man's worship of body and her mind would not mistake for love the dangerous awakening of her woman's sexuality.

FORE

Zulfaa tells me she loves Chicago winters because they are useful beyond design, accidentally; very much like the makeup-dust of her home, the savannah. When the winds of Chicago huff, Zulfaa's loosely tied head scarf absconds. When the winds of Chicago puff, Zulfaa's skirt rises to the occasion, flashing her ankles most seductively, before all present. When it snows, the flakes fall onto her lashes and flutter down to her cheeks when she bats her lids. Her audience is different every night as she spins her web of seduction with expertise. All of her conquests have no salvation for she is merciless in the way she brandishes fragility and flashes piety. Zulfaa is a peddler. Her goods are lust; she takes your lust and sells it back to you wrapped in red paper, tied with gold strings and with a sprinkle of glitter on top.

Zulfaa still goes on nightly hunts, and even though men are the casualty, the real and ever-elusive prey is her sexuality. She can't find it in penises big or small, wide or narrow. And each time, it takes a little more willpower to stop herself from convulsing in agony almost simultaneously as her partner reaches orgasm. When, however, the men like me, fail to deliver on the physical end of her private hell, she gives her mother a call and laughs as they ponder what Zulfaa's life would have been if she hadn't been purified of the sexual itch; if she hadn't been sent away to Chibok to get an education; if Boko Haram hadn't invaded her school; if she hadn't escaped, throwing herself from the moving terror mobile on the day of her kidnap; if she hadn't been paraded in front of the whole country as evidence that the government was "working"; if the government hadn't handed her over to the Americans as proof that "the good guys always win" and that "we do not negotiate with terrorists."

Tonight like other nights, I'll squeeze Zulfaa's hands as we brush past each other on the train. I'll watch as the sight of Zulfaa and the suggestion of her body under the artificial down of her winter jacket consumes a man's senses and I'll watch as she reels in the kill. I'll get off the train when they do and walk behind them on the street until I'm convinced that Zulfaa, my reluctant damsel, will live another day to grieve again, to share her mutilation, the gift that keeps on giving.

The Orphan's Daughter

Among my favorite childhood memories is story time with my mother.

Every few days, I would find myself sitting near the edge of Mommie's bed excitedly awaiting story time instructions. We didn't always use books. Most of the time we just used our imagination to tell each other stories. Sometimes I would freestyle a tale, usually about some happy elephant prancing about in a dream world. My stories were filled with dialogue and lots of "And then...and then...and then..." I enjoyed making my characters speak, and Mommie would listen intently until I finally lost my wind and had to concede to "The End!"

When it was Mommie's turn to tell a story, she would be so expressive and animated that it was easy to get lost in her words. Sometimes the story was all make-believe, coming true only at the end when she would reveal a gift of a small statuette that had been the story's protagonist all along. Like the time I was given a tiny glass pig after he had been the hero of his tale. Mommie had held him in her balled-up hand the whole time, presenting him to a squealing me who was so happy to meet a celebrity pig. Sometimes the stories were based on statues, and sometimes the stories were based on stories.

Mommie's background story is unbelievable. It always has been. And when she would present snippets of her life, in no particular order, I felt as if I had earned a piece of her bit by bit. Sometimes the stories were ironic, or funny, or painful—mentally and physically. Like the time Mommie told me the story of a fight in the orphanage. She and her friends played a game of Three Blind Mice with Joanie, a girl they disliked. When it was Joanie's turn to be the blind mouse, the other girls punched at her. This part of the story came complete with Mommie's extended fist coming toward me so animatedly that I was inadvertently knocked clean off the edge of her bed. I literally felt that story.

Other times, she would talk about her sister who had died at age eighteen. The stories would be so compelling and descriptive that I actually wept for that woman, because I knew I could never meet her.

Then there were times she pressed back to stories of Harlem when she was a small, barefoot Puerto Rican girl with a little brother and big sister roaming the streets begging for change. The three children had been left in an apartment following the death of their father and the nervous fleeing of their mother. These stories gave me the most of my Mommie. She was most vulnerable in these tales, often ending up in tears.

Story time was a thing that lasted us through my childhood up until it was almost time for me to leave for college. I was eighteen years old the last time I sat at the edge of Mommie's bed for a story. It was just two months later that her bed would be no more, and she was gone from this side of earth. But I had already been filled with so much of her. It is in the bits and pieces given to me at story time that I share this lifelong journey of tracing my mother's past, seeking and finding answers, looking for lineage, and learning myself.

Three Little Orphans

Three little orphans sit at the dock of a bay window whistling a familiar tune. It's the kind of window you always see in the movies, Mommie said. "The 'homes' in the movies must be real homes."

She never used the word orphanage; she always said "the home." St. Michael's Home for Children was a Catholic orphanage located at 1380 Arthur Kill Road on Staten Island, right by the big red dumpster. When I was in seventh grade, a teacher from Staten Island told me that NASA once reported that the dumpster was so big, it could be seen from the moon. My mom confirmed that the dumpster was the biggest, most impressive thing on Staten Island, especially on "Art-tu-keeel Road." Turns out the 'dumpster' was actually a 2,200 acre landfill hailed as the largest landfill in the world until its closure in 2001. It's a park now.

So there was an orphanage, a landfill, and about three hundred orphans on this major artery that runs along the South-west shore of Staten Island. To a young child, it must have looked so large, but it is only about 8.70 miles long and a million emotions away from home.

"We used to sit in that window on Saturdays and watch people get visited by their families," Mommie's story would begin. She told this story any time Otis Redding would come on the radio. "And we would sing *Sittin' in the mornin' sun/I'll be sittin' when the evenin' comes...*" Her voice perfectly melodic. When Redding got to the part about nothing changing, Mommie would stop and stare into any empty space in the room. A solemn look would encompass her, and she'd whistle. Whistle like it was everything in her. Whistle like it would bring her back to that bay window, and somehow this time, someone would be coming to visit her.

"We sat there every Saturday," she told me.

I would think about my Saturdays and how the only time I really spent by the window was to open it before weekly cleaning. Mommie would be downstairs with the radio blasted on WDAS, Philly's Classic Soul station. We kids would be upstairs with a combination of Soul Train and the latest rap album competing for loudest, with the smells of Pine-Sol and bleach permeating the air.

Mommie's adult Saturdays at that time consisted of waking up at 7 a.m. She would sit up in bed with one foot propped up on a nightstand that had a story of its own. Chain-smoking two-three cigarettes was an essential part of her morning ritual. She would then trade her nightgown for a bra, loose-fitting t-shirt, and cut-off stretch pants. Retreating to the living room, she would sit on the sofa with her music so loud that it would rattle the cheap windows of that barely two-story duplex that sat in the middle of the cul-de-sac-shaped street. After about an hour or so, she slid her darkened-from-walking-barefoot feet into a pair of worn flip-flops, grabbed her patch-work style leather pocketbook, and prepared on her way to the thrift shop of the day. From the back window of the house, I could see her trying to sneak away without having to take a child with her.

I would yell through the open window—"Wait for meeeeeeee!"

"I'm coming right back," Mommie would respond.

"No! That's what your Mamí told you! And she didn't come back! Don't leave meeeeeeeee!"

She would yell for me to hurry along, and I would race out of the house for our Saturday shopping trip.

One time Otis Redding came on the radio as soon as she turned the key into the ignition. We sat in the pebbled alleyway parking space beyond our little wired fence until the song was over. Then on our way we went.

Hwee, hwee, hwoo, hwoo, hwee, hwee, hwee, hwoo, hwoo...

Mommie's Sister

In traditional cases, one's mother's sister is regarded by the term aunt. Mommie's sister, Theresa, was an apparition the day that I met her. I know her only through my dimples that cratered Mommie's memories.

"I can't kick your ass the way I want to...you remind me too much of my sister," Mommie would yell at me whenever I did something wrong.

A certified boy mom for thirteen years before I was born, Mommie's only example of womanhood was her big sister. And so, in that regard, everything I did was reminiscent of her. Sometimes I wished I could have rolled myself into her just to make Mommie's smile more than a memory.

Mommie's sister was beautiful. I know this because I've seen pictures of her. Perfectly styled reddish-brown hair, a smile like pink roses in the springtime, light brown almond-shaped eyes, and a radiance you could feel just from her photo alone. I've not one day in my life lived up to that woman's outer glow.

But Mommie's odd comparisons came up in the weirdest of ways. When I was in trouble for something, Mommie's anger would soften when she looked into my round, dark brown eyes. The first time that happened I thought, "Good looking out, Theresa!" From then on, she was my guardian angel. I found out later that she was looking out for Mommie instead.

Theresa made frequent visits to our home. She had a favorite location—the entryway between the living room and the kitchen. I had never seen her, but Mommie would whiten and stare stunned into the entryway.

"I'm fucking up again," the story would always begin.

Mommie would swear that Theresa's apparition would visit to set her straight. This is the way I'm told this sisterly relationship worked before Theresa died. One to two years Mommie's senior, Theresa was, in Mommie's words, funny, sweet, extremely sensitive, and stern. She worked hard in her young age to help keep Mommie—the wild child—on track. But her earthly duties ended when she was only eighteen years old.

"You don't see my sister?" Mommie asked.

"No, I don't see anything."

"She's here."

"Is she talking to you?"

"No, she's not saying anything, but she's disappointed in me."

"What did you do?"

The room fell silent. And as sure as I knew that I was about to hear a story about Theresa, I did not. Instead, I watched a single tear drop from Mommie's eyes. She put her head down slightly, stuck her index finger into her freshly poured glass of Budweiser, and licked the foam from her knuckle. Head still lingering forward, her lips lunged toward the glass for a gulp. Fingers circled each other, fumbling for a Newport. A spark of light drew the nicotine into Mommie's premature, compromised lungs, and I was shooed away.

"Get outta here," Mommie said. "You know you can't be around cigarette smoke."

As I walked away opposite of Theresa's entryway, I could hear Mommie continue to fumble, this time for her stereo remote. WDAS blared out a tune from her teen years. And Theresa was with her, just like the old days.

The Candy Man

"You know, you don't truly recover after seeing someone get murdered," Mommie said. "But death doesn't scare me."

We were sitting on the front porch enjoying New Jersey's early spring breeze as clouds of smoke from Mommie's lips circled the stoop. Mount Holly Police Department had just broken up a vicious fight in which all of our neighborhood had front row access. No one was murdered that day, but Mommie's memory was triggered.

"You saw a murder," I screeched.

Mommie had seen lots of death. As a little girl she laughed before she knew her youngest sister's neck was snapped in midair while playing with her Papí. Another time, she watched her Papí push a chair toward an open window struggling to let air enter his asthmatic lungs when the chair flipped backwards. She watched her Mamí home abort more than two children in the bathtub. Mommie watched her sister, still too scared from institutionalized life, slowly die from not getting checked for what ended up being hepatitis. Mommie became a licensed practical nurse and then a hospice. She watched death happen like it was an important part of her life.

But this story was about the candy man.

The candy man was a slender black Latino who owned a corner store. It was not a candy shop, but that's all the niños of Spanish Harlem knew it to be.

"I saved up enough money for a big bag of candy," Mommie said.

This was a huge deal because on normal occasions, a tiny version of Mommie (she was only 4'11" as an adult) would sneak her candy away from the shop without getting caught. So, to be able to buy something gave her great joy.

"The candy man yelled at me. He told me to leave," she recalled. "I said, 'I just want some candy.' Then a guy I've never seen before threw a lot of candy at me, like a parade. I picked it up and asked for a bag. The candy man was crying, begging me to leave. I got my bag and started to walk out of the door."

Just like Mommie in the story, I didn't understand what was happening.

"And then the guy shot the candy man while I looked dead in his eyes. Maybe that's why death doesn't bother me."

Every time Mommie talked about death I would cry.

"Stop being a big baby. Everybody dies. I'm going to die," Mommie said every time the situation arose.

And I always walked away. I might look just like her but seeing through her eyes wasn't something I ever hoped for.

Thought for the day

Mommie kept a pocket-sized notebook for her thoughts. Each evening her brain would unravel into twisted words. We were an unwilling audience, her children, given a small piece of her story at prime time.

"Analyze this," she always began.

Her beautiful handwriting horizontally filled the tiny vertical pages. For as much as she refused to follow the rules, her writing was no different—no form or pattern, no understandable rhyme or reason—just words.

She considered herself no poet, did not claim to be a writer, just a thinker. This was thinking out loud. Each evening, after she read from her nightstand podium, she would confetti the paper.

"That's just the thought for the day," she'd say as she would turn those thoughts into dust.

On the day she herself was dust, I grabbed her notebook, scrambling for her thoughts, but she left none behind. Only the days are still here.

Bittersweet

The uneven pavement between the school and Mum's shop seemed shorter that day as we were all enthralled in our own mini-dramas.

I was still reeling from the day's events and trying hard not to let it show. Marva hustled to finish her lolly. Anticipating the tongue lashing waiting for her if Mum saw it, I suppose. The blue stickiness started escaping her hands as it melted, trickling freely down the length of her arm to her elbow. Her white shirt would surely be irrevocably soiled soon. Droplets of blue had already started forming a polka dot pattern on the stiff pocket near the school insignia. A right mess both she and Carl were, and Mumà would most definitely have something to say about it.

Carl was sucking on his suckabag with all of the classlessness that Mum feared was predetermined by his 'hard hair' as she called it. It was low to his head, but peasy. "No brotherly love between his strands," a couple of our uncles often joked. It was sandy-colored with a reddish tint like Daddy's was before the grays staged the coup. Daddy's was soft and curly—an almost unnatural-looking curl, like a granny with sponge rollers, but it grew that way. Ma Sugar used to say that was the cocoa panyol in him. She always seemed so pleased to say it. It dripped off of her tongue onto her lips like sweet cane juice. The panyol canceled the bitter cocoa that traveled down the bloodline.

She always emphasized the panyol as though it was the sound of redemption. The panyol kept his skin light enough to be Trini white-ish. He was country club light and just as long as he married right, no one would notice the traces of cocoa in his substantial lips and broad nose.

***

I was there the day they brought Carl home from the hospital. Ma Sugar was sitting in her rocking chair on the veranda. The one to the back of the house because the breeze there was nicer she said. What she meant was she didn't have to see the new neighbors. She was convinced the neighborhood was getting bad. She would arm herself with her heavy-duty housecoat, newspapers, and a pink plastic fly swatter. The fly swatter was for Miss Rosie, the domestic that worked for her. She would sit, but Miss Rosie always stood. When they first moved in with us after Pops died, I would offer Miss Rosie a seat. I never noticed her standing at Ma and Pops' place. Maybe that's because Pops was still alive. He had a way of reigning in Ma. Nobody ever says, but I think he used to give her some good licks. Cousin Martin said that's "what mouthy red women" would get back in those days. "A woman had to know her place or get knocked back into it." He'd smile a broad smile. I'd always spit in his Mauby when he came to dinner.

The first few times I offered Miss Rosie a seat, Ma gave me a cut eye that would rock your soul. I didn't understand though, and then one day she exclaimed, "Let her stand! That's her damn job!" I was startled and ran off. I could hear her calling behind me, "Yuh can't encourage these people to be lazy!"

She must've thought the new neighbors were lazy as well. When their gardeners arrived or their trash was put out late, she scoffed loudly.

As far as I knew, most of the people moving in were economists at Central Bank and high-level executives in the local banking scene, but Ma said they were darkening our doorstep. Mummy and Daddy just laughed her off. I never did get the joke.

***

The day that they brought Carl home from WestShore hospital, he was beautifully round with the slightest yellowish tan like a ball of ripe plantain. They brought him outside for Ma Sugar to see. She furrowed her brows as she examined the tops of his ears and his tiny knuckles.

She rubbed her hand over his soft head. She steupsed loudly—the smack of saliva and air against her dentures was jarring—as she declared, "This one will not play in sun or let this hair get too long."

There was no sweetness dripping onto her lips then. There was no panyol to emphasize, just bitter cocoa. The bitterness that filled her mouth when she insisted Miss Rosie stand. Miss Rosie who wiped her behind, cooked her low-sodium meals, and traveled from D'abadie every Monday morning with a week's worth of clean clothes because she knew she'd have to carry them all back home dirty on Saturday morning. Miss Rosie whose aching knees were braced because she too was getting old. Miss Rosie whose shiny clear skin was slick on top like the cocoa tea she snuck me on the mornings Mum was running late. We dare not let Ma see.

That day, it was those same gentle, yet feeble hands that channeled Pops and knocked Ma straight across the back veranda just after lunch. I heard a loud lashing sound. I'd been curled up with my laptop on the old sofa in the lounge off of the veranda. I was falling deeper and deeper into a hair video spiral on YouTube. All of my panyol doesn't seem to make my hair any more manageable than Carl's. Most days, like then, it sits on top of my head in an unruly ponytail. I was in desperate search of a style that would insulate me from Ma's constant comments about how pretty I would be if only I'd properly straighten my hair. Maybe if I'd braided it like the girls from Laventille—the ghetto—she'd stop talking to me altogether, I thought. Wouldn't that have been a treat? I'd only been back home a day and a half from uni and she had already mentioned it ten times. The jarring lash cut through my trance like a whip in mid-air.

I rushed toward the door to find Miss Rosie standing there looking stunned. She had apparently reached for one of the cookies she baked at Ma's request and Ma swatted her hand with that pink plastic fly swatter. The stunned look on Miss Rosie's face only lasted a split second. I was frozen in the doorway. Miss Rosie was lunged toward Ma and raffed her up by the neck of her housecoat.

Ma was still yelling, "Blasted thief!" I'm not sure where Miss Rosie found the strength or if Ma really understood what was happening, but she reached back in time, whoosh Ma went flying. Scrambling to break her fall, she jerked her head as she hit the rocking chair and blood started to trickle down the back of her neck.

The anger on Miss Rosie's face turned to fright as I dialed 811 for the ambulance. She stood there—still—behind the rocking chair, and suddenly grabbed her chest. I saw her body slide down the wall, but by the time I made it through the sliding doors she was in a heap on the floor. I touched her—she was gone. Ma also seemed to be gone.

I wasn't quite sure what I was doing. I called Daddy and he came right home from the office, a two-minute drive. He determined that Miss Rosie had passed, but Ma was still holding on faintly. Apparently, "them mouthy red women" don't die just so. She held on until we made it to the hospital, but not much longer. Daddy stayed with her to wait for his sisters and cousins. In all the commotion, we hadn't thought to call Mum. She was at her tea shop all day. Usually, Daddy was the one to check in on Ma and Miss Rosie during the day. Ma and all that came with her was his responsibility. He asked me to go collect Marva and Carl from school and take them straight to the shop.

***

As we strolled through the ice blue tinted glass doors, the place was filled. Mum came rushing over to us, throwing her eyes hard at Marva's blue lips and patterned pocket, making big eyes at me and then at Carl's hand—the dripping suckabag leaking onto her shop floor. She ushered us with a hard shove into the backroom out of earshot of the customers.

"Mariah! Why do they look like vagabonds? What are you all doing here in the middle of the day?" she yelled.

I could feel all six of their eyes trained on me, but before I could get a word out, Mum reached around me and slapped Carl upside his head.

"Why are you walking around with your hair unbrushed? Eh? Why is it rolling up like this?"

My legs gave way under me. Maybe it was the dizziness of the day. Maybe it was the bitterness of her tone. When I came to, they were all sitting there drinking cocoa tea.

Things I Can't Outrun

A slight mist is suspended in the early morning air. The sun is just waking up. I swallow back a yawn as I stretch. There are a few hundred runners taking their positions at the starting line. In this space, there is an unvoiced hierarchy.

The fast runners, the ones who might actually win, are at the front, right beneath the banner. Their faces carry looks of determination, even though this is just a charity run, they approach it with the seriousness of the Olympic Trials. After them are those who consider themselves to be competitive but usually finish just barely in the top ten of their age groups. Then there are the runners who simply enjoy running. They wear obnoxious fanny packs with water bottles attached and listen to music on their earbuds as they jog. Many of them take selfies as they wait for the race to begin. Way in the back are the walkers. They chat in clusters of mostly middle-aged women. Some push strollers, and one even sips on a latte. The crowd is mostly white, with only a few specks of color.

Though I have been running since middle school, the charity road race crowd is still new to me. In high school, I was a sprinter. My favorite distance had been the 400m dash. I had owned that distance, having broken a long-held record at my high school. I was even fast enough to be awarded a scholarship to University of Georgia in Athens. Well, that was before things fell apart.

I do a semi jog in place, waiting for the announcements to finish up. There is a chill in the early March air, and I rub my arms. This race, The March with Heart 5K, like the dozen or so others I had run in the last year, is my attempt at getting back my stride. Before my first road race almost a year ago, it had been years since I had run at all.

The announcer calls out the locations of the water stops. To my left, a blonde woman attempts to position herself at the front of the starting line. She pushes past me, stepping squarely on my left foot. I stare at her, expecting an acknowledgment of her mistake, but she looks me up and down, appraising me with her fog gray eyes, and simply states, "Oh," before continuing on her way to the front. I want to say, "I know you didn't just step on my shoe and not apologize." Yet I know that in this space, I will be the one villainized, painted as just another angry Black woman breaking the serenity of this peaceful event.

From her position, only a few yards ahead of me, I can see her clearly. She's thin as a rail, her arms and legs the width of twigs. She wears her long bleached blonde hair pulled in a ponytail. On her feet are the shoes I have been coveting for months. The ones that Eliud Kipchoge wore to finish a marathon, 26.2 miles in under two hours. These shoes, as ugly as they are, cost $250. These are the shoes she used to step on my outdated, nearly worn out, $50 on clearance Adidas. I'm not pissed because she stepped on my shoe, I'm pissed because in the few seconds that she looked me up and down, taking in my shoes, maybe even the complexion of my skin, she decided that I wasn't worthy of an apology or even an acknowledgment. She looked at me and decided she could look through me.

I had planned to take it easy, to use this race as a training run, but in that moment a switch went off. My anger needs an outlet, and just like in so many other moments in my life, I decide to channel my anger into the race.

The announcer counts down, and a loud honk from the bullhorn marks the start of the race. I start to run. I steady my breathing and affirm to myself that I will actually compete today in a way I haven't in years.

In the years since high school, eight to be exact, I can still hear Coach Barnard's voice in my head. Whenever I would race the 1600m, which I hated, he would advise, "Start out slow. Use this first part to get your stride. Save something, always save a little something." Thinking of this, I run the first mile nice and easy. Soon, the faster runners separate themselves from the pack and there are only maybe ten of us spaced out on the road. We pass groups of spectators ringing bells, taking pictures. Some hold handmade banners. I try not to look at the crowds, instead focusing on my cadence. The sound of my steady footfalls calms me down.

We pass the water stop at mile marker 1, and I can see the blonde just ahead of me. I remember Coach's words, "The middle of the race is where you get your stride. This is where y'all fools try to zoom out. Stay focused! You got to stay focused!" I decide to overtake the blonde. With a little effort, I am shoulder-to-shoulder with her. Then I pass her, surprising myself. I can feel her energy shift. Her indignation is palpable. I can feel her eyes staring at the back of my head.

The hill is coming up. I have run through Piedmont Park enough to anticipate it. At mile 2, I let her pass me, knowing that I need to save a little something, as Coach Barnard always said. We get to the hill and I can sense her energy wane. The hill is brutal and seems to last forever.

My "little something" kicks in. I swing my arms, tighten my glutes, and push myself up the hill. My heart is beating in my ears, my lungs burn, and my legs feel heavy. I breathe through it, trying to keep steady breaths. The top of the hill is a little victory, from there I can allow my established momentum and gravity to pull me toward the finish line. I begin to wonder how far behind me she is, but I remember another one of Coach's oft-repeated phrases. "This is your race! Don't worry 'bout nobody else...your race to win or your race to lose!"

I push myself a little more. "Give it all you got...don't hold nothing back once you see that finish line." My chest hurts. My lungs are on fire, but I breathe through the pain. The runner from high school, the one who had been asleep for so long, wakes up. Just a few yards left. I see a few male runners ahead of me. *Am I the only woman up this far?* I focus on the finish line, now just a few feet away. I give one last push, running under the banner that marks the end of the race. There are crowds of families cheering, and more homemade banners. The announcer is calling out names, but I can't hear him over the crowd.

Did I just do what I think I did?

I see Jamal waiting for me. He's all smiles, wearing black jogging pants, a hoodie, and his retro J's. He's holding a cold bottle of water and a banana.

"Hey...that was amazing. I'm glad I didn't go use the bathroom. I would have missed you. Damn, you were running like you stole something." He laughs. I walk a little away from the crowd. The adrenaline has worn off, replaced with the pain in my right hip that has been nagging me lately. I take a few sips of water, try to regain my composure. Sweat drips down my face. I know I look like a hot mess.

"You okay?" Jamal asks.

I nod. "Yeah, I'm just a little shook."

The recreational runners are coming across the finish line now, greeted with cheers and applause.

"You know you won, right? The announcer pointed you out as the female winner."

"For real?"

Jamal nods, smiles.

"Well, don't look so impressed. This is a charity race, not exactly the Olympics," I say, looking around at the crowd. I ran well, but *fast* only in comparison to the runners present, who are mostly well past their prime.

We've been friends since the day I saw him handing a homeless man two organic Fuji apples that he pulled from a Whole Foods bag. I was exiting the store myself, experiencing buyer's remorse about two bags of groceries that had somehow cost over a hundred dollars. The man smelled like a portable toilet, yet Jamal smiled, gave him the apples and a card to his community outreach center.

I liked the fact that his work had meaning, giving back to the community. I liked his endless supply of hoodies and that he was two chicken sandwiches away from a dad-bod. Unlike Fabian. Fabian who spent more time in the mirror than I did. Fabian who got pissy when I refused to take "artistic semi-nudes" with him for his Instagram account. After we broke up, he took the photos alone, posting his chiseled abs and sinewy quads greased up with baby oil, his peen concealed by some type of loincloth.

"No cap! I can't believe you did it." He looks a little in awe. "You know, these races are kinda fun. You just might get me to start running. But y'alls shoes are so ugly."

I try to stretch my tight hip, wincing a little at the effort. Jamal hands me the banana. "Maybe you should eat something."

"Thanks," I say, taking a bite. His concern, and even just the fact that he's here at all, reminds me of my first road race last year. Fabian promised to cheer me on, but never showed up.

I feel a tap on my shoulder. I turn to see Shelly, a short brunette I met through the RUNATL group over a year ago. The first time I met her, she invited me to her apartment right off The Beltline and gave me a pair of Lululemon running shorts. "The color just washes me out," she said. The bright yellow shorts had become a favorite of mine, and if it hadn't been cold out this morning, I would have worn them today.

Shelly gives me a sweaty hug. Her blue shorts expose her chicken legs, which are turning red in the cool air. "Nakisha! I heard you won!" Shelly is the only white person I have ever met who has come close to pronouncing my name correctly and has never once asked, "Can I call you Kiki?"

"Have you met Melodie?" she asks. "Come meet her, she's great. We all thought she would take it this year." Before I know it, Shelly is pulling me toward the fog-eyed blonde. "Hey Melodie, this is Nakisha."

Melodie gives me a tight smile.

"Great job out there," she says with slight derision. "I started cramping up on that hill," she says, an excuse for her performance. "I knew I should've taken my magnesium this morning."

"Yes, that hill was a killer," Shelly comments. "It almost got me too."

"Where are you from? Are you Kenyan?" Melodie asks, examining me.

I wonder for a second if she's joking, but she looks at me calmly, expecting an answer.

"No. I was born at Grady Memorial Hospital." I let the silence sit between us.

"I mean your parents?"

"They're from Decatur."

The announcer calls everyone to attention. "Okay, ladies and gentlemen! We have crunched our numbers. We still have some walkers out there on the course, but we'll begin announcing the winners." He starts with the men, calling out John Rono, a tall African man, as the male winner. Followed by Brett Woods and Nicolas Johnson as second and third place. They go up to the podium and receive medals and gift certificates to a local running store.

"Okay, now for the ladies. All right please forgive me, I know I'm going to butcher this," he says with a laugh. "In first place, we have Naa-ke-shee Rhodes."

I go up to the podium for my medal and gift certificate, suddenly realizing that I might be able to get some of those hideous shoes after all.

***

Running used to be as large a part of me as the color of my skin. The track was my second home, and the girls on my high school track team were like family. Coach Barnard watched over us like a mother and a father rolled into one.

I respected Coach Barnard's rigid training style. He didn't give a fuck about feelings, and I respected that. "Don't stop when you're tired. Stop when I say you're done, damn it," he often said. Yet, he peppered his harsh truisms with moments of gentle encouragement. "I'm only pushing you because I believe in you. If I didn't believe in you, I'd let you do whatever the hell you wanted, kick you off the team, and let you be someone else's problem."

I had hoped to find that same sense of security and familiarity in college. My first day on the track, I was shocked by how very white my team was. The girls wore their hair in high ponytails and giggled with each other over jokes that I felt excluded from. The head coach, Coach Harris, was so pale that he turned red in the sun.

There were a handful of Black girls on the team, but most were immigrants or the children of immigrants. My experience was so different from theirs. We tried to find common ground, but it felt forced. I did make one friend on the team. Simone was a Black girl that came from a small town in southern Georgia and felt as out of place on the oversized campus as I did.

I struggled to adapt to Coach Harris' training. Looking back, I guess I felt like I had to prove something. I would go all out at the start and become winded not even halfway through the drills. "Slow the hell down, Rhodes," he would shout, yet his tough love lacked the sense of understanding I had experienced with Coach Barnard. I could feel myself failing, something that I had never experienced before. I started training harder, running in the morning before morning practice and late at night while my roommate, Ashleigh, was sleeping or out partying.

The depression snuck up on me. I would cry during solo runs sometimes, allowing the tears to flow, mix with my sweat and cover the front of my tank tops. Yet, my body stubbornly refused to cooperate, in more ways than one. The team nutritionist had a closed-door meeting with me about what he called "our nutrition goals." His goal was for me to work on "reducing body fat percentage in order to improve your aerobic threshold." This was the first time I had ever heard the word "fat" used in reference to me. Before UGA, I wore an XS or small, and even with a few extra pounds, I still wore a size small, or maybe a medium. He gave me print-outs that listed red foods, which I should limit, and green foods which I could eat in moderation. "Gotta limit that fried chicken," he had said with a laugh. His attempt at a joke.

I followed the eating plan but didn't lose any weight. That's when the exhaustion started. After running, I had little energy left to study or, on some days, even attend class. One day, after falling asleep in class and being woken up by a professor, I realized I was drowning. Later that same day, I found out I wouldn't be allowed to compete in the upcoming spring season.

"We think we should give your body a little more time to acclimate," Coach Harris had said.

I had left for UGA confident, happy, and sure of myself, yet returned six months later, defeated. I transferred to Georgia State, attending classes on their campus in the middle of downtown. I decided to major in Education, envisioning myself teaching kindergarten to a room full of bright-eyed five-year-olds. I stopped running.

During my junior year, I found out that I had an underactive thyroid. The doctor who diagnosed me was a kind brown-skinned woman who asked me a series of questions about my energy levels, weight, and mood. "I'm surprised no one has ever checked your thyroid levels in the past," she said kindly. "Don't worry," she assured, "nothing a couple of pills can't fix." She chuckled.

Since that day, I have taken a small pill that regulates my thyroid hormones, and sometimes as I shake the small white pill from my prescription bottle, I wonder how different my life would be if someone had asked the right questions that first year of college.

***

Jamal drives a no-nonsense black Toyota Camry. Inside is clean and always recently vacuumed, another thing I appreciate about him. "Where to?" he asks, backing his car out of his parking spot. "We're going to brunch at my grandma's house, but I gotta head home and shower first."

My phone rings. The caller ID reads: MAMA.

"I heard you won!" she's practically screaming into my ear. "Jamal sent me a photograph. This just warms my heart."

Jamal has only met my mother three times, yet he texts her occasionally.

He texts my dad too. I have seen long paragraphs from him lambasting the President.

"Kisha, I been texting you for the past week! You coming to brunch or not?" My grandmother is now screaming into the phone.

"Yes, Granny."

"Don't you 'yes Granny' me, little girl. Y'all are always on these phones and can't spare a moment to text me back."

"But Granny, I did text you back."

My grandmother hardly knows how to operate her phone outside of making calls. She is always sending me pictures unintentionally or texting the wrong grandchild.

"Hmmm...well what time are you coming? This food gone get cold waiting on y'all."

If I know my Grandmother, I know that she has likely not even started cooking.

"We're on the way," I lie. "Granny, remember Jamal is coming and he doesn't eat any pork."

"Who's this Jamal?"

"Granny, you've met Jamal before, remember at Thanksgiving?"

"Lil girl, I can't keep track of all the men y'all done brought into this house."

I have introduced my grandmother to only two men, Fabian and Jamal. She must be confusing me with my sister Anika, who has a revolving door when it comes to men.

"So why don't he eat no pork? He ain't one of them damn vegans is he?"

"Well, no he's not vegan. He's Muslim."

"Muslim? It don't surprise me you bringing home a Muslim. Sheila," she says addressing my mother, "see what happens when you don't raise those kids in church."

It's true my mother hadn't "raised us up in church." My mother considers herself a spiritualist, looking for and finding the truth in all religions. Instead of baptisms, she had African naming ceremonies for me, my brother, and my little sister, complete with a Yoruba priest.

"Soon he's gonna have her all covered up, selling bean pies by the overpass!"

"Listen, I gotta go. See y'all soon," I say. I can hear her fussing as I hang up.

I had met Jamal only a month before inviting him to have Thanksgiving with my family. I was attracted to his kindness and interested in his work. I had been looking for a way to give back, and soon began spending Saturday mornings at the outreach center off of Pryor Street, serving up meals to the homeless.

He had mentioned being Muslim casually, as if mentioning his shoe size, and I didn't think much of it at first. I honestly didn't know much about the religion, other than the fact that they don't eat pork, and their women covered their hair. Over time, he confessed that he hadn't always been committed to his faith; that he used to drink and have girlfriends in his twenties, but was now recommitted to his faith and prayed five times a day. I found this unbelievable at first, but I walked in on him one day at the outreach center, behind his desk, prostrating on an embroidered rug. I respected this about him. Yet it wasn't something I could ever imagine myself doing.

When he told me most of his family lived in Chicago, I urged him to spend Thanksgiving with us.

"I don't know. You sure they won't get the wrong idea about us?"

"What idea would that be?" I teased.

He shrugged, turning serious for a minute. "I made a promise to God that I wouldn't know a woman intimately again until after I marry her. I'm not making any assumptions, just letting you. There's only so far our relationship can go."

"We're just friends," I said. "Right?"

He nodded.

Eventually, our friendship developed further. Now we spend every weekend together, and call and text each other throughout the week. The first race Jamal came to was a New Year's resolution run that I nonchalantly mentioned I was running in. He surprised me at the finish line, a cup of hot cocoa in his hand.

We had only kissed once, a late-night goodbye a few weeks ago that had turned more affectionate than anticipated. His lips were parted slightly, and I allowed my tongue to greet his. Abruptly, he ended the kiss. I was still a little out of breath when he pulled himself from me, said a hasty goodbye, and left.

He later texted me apologizing, and we haven't spoken about it since.

***

We enter my Grandmother's home and are greeted by the smell of bacon cooking. My sister is on the sofa, holding my nephew, Nathan, who is barely five months old. He lies sleeping in my sister's arms. I kiss him on the cheek, enjoying his baby smell, and give my sister a sideways hug.

"Good morning," Jamal greets her.

"Hey," she responds.

If my mother and grandmother are the most unalike mother and daughter pair I know, my own mother and Anika take a close second place. Anika has a sew-in weave that flows down her back. Today she wears eyelashes longer than my index finger. My mother has had locs since she was pregnant with me and doesn't wear any makeup besides some tinted lip gloss, occasionally.

We enter the kitchen to find my grandmother and mother fussing at each other in the kitchen.

"Sheila, you done burned that bacon!"

"It isn't burnt," my mother replies, exasperated.

"Good morning," I announce.

"Well look at you. You cleaned up pretty good." She gives me a hug. Jamal had waited in his car parked outside my apartment, as I showered and changed out of my sweaty leggings and into dark jeans and a sweater.

"Hey, Jamal." She embraces him as well.

My grandmother sits at the table, frowning at the "burned" bacon. I lean over to give her a hug, and she looks us up and down.

"You must be the Muslim," she says to Jamal.

"Mama!" My mother is embarrassed.

But Jamal only laughs. "Yes Ma'am."

I often wonder why my grandmother is so adamant about having the whole family over, when she usually spends most of the time fussing at everyone.

The table spread is almost complete. There's baked french toast, quiche, salmon croquettes, biscuits, home fries, and fresh fruit plus the bacon that she still sits frowning at.

"Where's Daddy and Dionte?" I ask.

"They're in the basement. Can you go get them?"

Jamal and I head down to the basement, which has been finished and turned into a TV room. There's a sofa sectional, and here my father and brother sit watching something on the big screen television.

"Hey there, baby girl! I heard your good news."

I kiss my father on the cheek. My father is the yin to my mother's yang. He wasn't 100% sold on the spirituality, but he left her to her candles and crystals.

"I remember how fast you used to be on that track. You were like Flo-Jo out there," he smiles at the memory.

"I'm not that fast anymore, but it was fun."

"She did great," Jamal says.

My father has this way of examining your face and finding the truth in your eyes, rather than your words. He studies Jamal, and gives me a knowing smirk.

"Sup, sis? Hey, Jamal." Dionte nods in our direction, barely taking his eyes off of the TV screen. Dionte is in his third year at Morehouse College. He wears jeans and a Tupac t-shirt, his short locs braided back away from his forehead.

"What's this?" I ask. The screen is on a Black man seated at what looks like a low-budget news desk.

"It's this news show that comes on YouTube. Citizen World News."

"It's not one of those broadcasts filled with conspiracy theories, is it?"

Dionte rolls his eyes at me. "Y'all need to wake up. This is the news they don't want you to see on TV."

The seated man has a somber tone to his voice. "The footage I'm about to show you is very disturbing, and it hurts me that I have to show it to you."

"Let me guess, he has footage of aliens?" I say.

"No, that was last week," my father chuckles.

Dionte ignores us, his eyes glued to the screen.

The announcer continues. "This young man was jogging in a city called Brunswick, Georgia, when he was chased, hunted down like an animal, in a pickup truck driven by two white men..."

The word "jogging" catches my attention, and I'm drawn into the program. Soon, the image of the bootleg news desk is replaced by a video of a young Black man jogging on a tree-lined street.

Jamal stands near me, his eyes on the screen.

We see a white pickup truck stop directly in front of him. The camera pans away, and when it returns, a white man runs with a shotgun pointed at the young man. I want to turn away, but I can't. I'm praying that this won't end how I think it will. In the video they struggle for the gun, there's one gunshot, and then two more. The young man tries to run away, but falls to the ground, blood on his shirt.

"No, oh my God!" I yell out. I'm horrified by what I've just seen. I cover my mouth with my hands.

"The men who hunted down and shot this young Black king, like an animal, are still free. I want to make it clear that no arrest has been made."

"That can't be true!" Without realizing it, I'm yelling. "They couldn't have just shot him like that on video and gotten away with it, and why haven't we heard anything about it? Brunswick isn't that far from here!"

The host is already on to the next report. He talks about a new virus coming out of China, saying it was created in a lab in Wuhan. Dionte turns off the TV. I wish he had done that before that video was shown.

"It could be true. Sis, you know they don't care about us."

Jamal puts his arm around me. "Kisha, if the video's been released, the killers will be held accountable. In these situations, we gotta be patient." I can see the burning rage in his eyes, the tension in his jaw.

At the table, I pick over my food. I can't eat. Everyone has a different opinion on why the killers haven't been arrested, or even if they ever will be.

"He shoulda known better than running in that neighborhood," Granny says.

I'm shocked by her words.

"Now, Ma, don't say that. A person can run wherever they want," my father says, taking a bite of bacon.

"Can. That don't mean should. You see what happened, don't you?"

Everyone has an opinion. Jamal tries to politely disagree with her, but she's staunch in her position.

"Does that mean I shouldn't have run today? There were mostly white people out there this morning." I think about Melodie and the way she looked at me. Her face stated that I didn't belong. I feel a suppressed rage bubbling up inside of me.

Granny shrugs and continues eating.

The images from the video replay in my mind. The truth that he could have been me sits uncomfortably in my throat.

"You know, the sad part is, even if the killers are arrested, that won't bring him back," my mother says.

Everyone is silent for a moment. I stare at the food on my plate.

"You better eat something after all that running you been doing," Granny urges.

I take a few bites of quiche, but I find it difficult to swallow.

After brunch, I help clean up. Jamal is on the sofa, watching ESPN with my father. Granny, tired out from the cooking, goes to lie down. My mother is making fresh-pressed juice, grinding ginger and carrots. The sound of the juicer almost wakes my nephew.

Anika asks how Jamal is in bed.

"We haven't done anything. I told you we're just friends." She raises her eyebrow at me and shrugs.

"Yea, Nathan's daddy and I were just friends too," she laughs.

I Google his name. I find his obituary alongside a picture of his smiling face. It speaks of his kindness and humility. He loved to tell jokes and played sports, football and basketball. He had attended college. He was only twenty-five years old.

***

Jamal is dropping me off at home. He pulls in front of my apartment and turns the car off. We sit quietly, listening to the engine tick down.

"So, when's the next race?" he asks.

I'm silent. What if it had been me gunned down on a run, my brown skin taken as a menacing threat?

When I got back into running, it had become a means of escape. My training was erratic. Some days I'd run two miles, some days ten. While running, I could push everything from my mind. Mile after mile, nothing mattered except the pounding of my feet and the rhythm of my breath. It was a place where I could pretend the ugliness of the world didn't exist.

I don't think I can ever be carefree while running again. Not after seeing that video.

I shrug. A few tears trail down my cheeks.

Jamal gives me a hug, enclosing me in the warmth of his hoodie.

Barricade

For children, time is like the stretch of the ocean before a sailor preparing to embark. There are days, hours, moments to fill to break up the journey. With children, if no one tells them what to do with their time, they find ways to occupy it. For twin brother and sister, Flint and Amara, along with their neighbor Ebony, they spent their time as only children can, with adventure and imagination.

They'd play cops and robbers, hopping fences into other people's backyard, dodging Rottweilers chained to a stake. Sometimes they'd see who could climb the valley oak the highest. To them, it was a fortress surrounded by lava, and they'd compete to see who'd hold onto the branch the longest. If you fell, you'd be engulfed in the lava, and sometimes break a bone. One day, Ebony and Amara created a new game.

It involved the chain-linked fence in the twin's back yard. The fence had no bar at the top to keep it up, so it sagged, and because of this, Ebony and Amara perched at opposite ends, and it bent to their weight. When they wanted, they bounced, allowing the fence to sink, then spring them back up. Flint wandered from the side of the house as he finished his popsicle. He stopped before the girls could see him and listened to their conversation.

"Did you know blood is blue, but it turns red when the air hits it?" Amara asked.

"Now how would I know that? I've only ever seen the red kind," Ebony said.

"It's true," Amara said, nodding.

"How do you know it's blue if you've never seen it?" asked Ebony.

"I heard it. Doctors know about it," Amara replied.

Ebony studied her a minute and saw that Amara believed. Ebony wasn't so quick to believe something just because someone told her it was true.

Ebony hit Amara's shoulder. "Come on let's bounce."

Amara counted to three then pushed down. They bounced once, then twice, then the fence slowed down as did the girl's laughter. Flint walked over to the bottom of the gate. He squinted up at them, one hand covering his eyes, blocking out the sun. The syrup from the popsicle dried on his skin, leaving blue lines up to his elbows, resembling veins.

"Can I play?" he asked.

"Go away," Amara said, straightening her old Sunday dress. Her mom tried to throw it away many times, claiming she'd outgrown it, but Amara found a use for it. She often paired it with tennis shoes and wore it out to play. Ebony didn't understand why her friend wanted to wear a dress every day, but then again, Ebony stuck to cutoff shorts and her favorite Tweety Bird t-shirt.

"Come on," Flint said, "I'll give you a piece of gum." He searched his cargo shorts pockets.

It wasn't that Amara didn't want him to join, but it brought her satisfaction to know that she played a game he couldn't. The fence had been collapsing for a while, but she discovered this game, not him.

"You know he's not going to leave until we let him play," Ebony mentioned.

"Fine, come on," Amara said, not realizing that he would offset the equal distribution of weight on each side.

Flint climbed up, face flushed, panting with his tongue out and to the side of his mouth. He settled between the girls, as did his sweet grassy scent from playing outside all day.

"On three, we push down. Remember to hold on tight on the way up," Amara explained.

The twin's neighbor, Mrs. Patricia, watched all this happening from her yard as she sipped iced tea at her table. Mrs. Patricia was always in her backyard at that table, staring off at what the kids thought was nothing. She usually kept to herself, but her voice reached over to them that day.

"You kids are gonna get hurt," she warned.

They glared over at the lady they knew as the neighbor with the straw hat. In this deadlocked moment, the kids thought about whether to listen to her or not. They knew to listen to their elders, but there were hardly ever any elders around. A heaviness descended on all of them, what they later learned was their intuition urging them to realize something.

Used to supervising herself, Amara felt that what adults said carried no importance. She turned back to them and said, "Three."

Pushing down with the added weight allowed them to plunge closer to the ground, but just before touching it, the fence catapulted them into the air. Their grip ripped from the metal, and they flung into the sky. Beads of sweat on their skin evaporated as they ascended past the power lines ornamented with Chuck Taylors. At their peak, they grabbed bits of cloud, and it dissolved in their hands like cotton candy on the tongue. Mrs. Patricia stood and squinted up at their bodies plastered against the sapphire sky.

The kids beheld the castles of clouds surrounding them. Maybe it was because she was closer to the sun, but Ebony saw everything clearly, especially her best friends. From up here, Ebony acknowledged that she looked forward to the knock at the door from the twins every day. With the sunset came a night of spoon-feeding her dad yogurt mixed with crushed pills and getting up every few hours to check on him. The twin's faces lifted the denseness of the night. Ebony wanted to tell them this, but the words couldn't rise from her, so she looked down at their neighborhood. From up high, it had a golden hue.

Amara recalled the time her family went on a road trip to the beach. When they still did spur-of-the-moment trips, when they were still together. They drove with the windows down, so Amara continuously removed hair from her face to see her parents in the front, holding hands. Shuggie Otis's Freedom Flight repeated on the cassette player as they flew by town after town.

Once there, she couldn't take her eyes off the body of water in the distance. Flint, along with other kids, played in the water while Amara sat in the sand watching the waves roll toward her and crash to the shore then pulled back out. Eventually, Flint realized that Amara wasn't around, so he'd run to her reporting on how fun it was, asking her to join.

The clouds around her now looked just like the waves breaking on the beach except they have paused here never settling. Flint found his favorite castle, the largest one complete with a throne. He attempted to go to it but found his body moved at a slower pace from up here.

The kids realized there is more time within the expanse of time they already have. Slipping into a sliver of a second, they glanced at the past, assured because it brought them here. It made them certain of what was to come because, if they reached this form of paradise, there must be other forms out there. They got so high. And no matter how much they explained that memory, no one could grasp the magnitude of that day. People listened, but with the same response of telling your dream to someone. Like they are twice removed, or it's not real, but even though they couldn't tangibly show someone, it determined every decision they made later in life.

Sometimes when Amara looked at Flint, she saw that moment replaying in the reflection of his eyes. If it weren't for what happened next, the three of them would forever try to reach those heights again. They came down, hard. So hard and fast, no one had the opportunity to grab hold of the gate, so the jagged top sliced the backside of their legs. On their backs, they looked up at where they once were. The gate meant to keep the neighbors separated failed, and the children collected themselves in Mrs. Patricia's yard. Amara sat up and saw that she was not bleeding yet, but the stinging started at the clean cuts running from her thighs to her ankles. *The blood must still be blue*, she thought.

The gate meant to keep the neighbors separated failed and the kids were now Mrs. Patricia's problem. Ebony remained on the cool grass, focusing on the fact that Mrs. Patricia's grass was always green while everyone else's yard was like hay. What made her grass so different when the chain-linked fence was the only thing that separated the yards? Blood emerged from the slices, and Ebony sat up to wipe the lines, revealing pink meat where skin once protected.

"Where did you guys go? What was it like up there? I've never seen anything like it. Are you all right?" Mrs. Patricia asked the entire way over to them.

Flint's lip shook and his face crumbled into a cry. He didn't realize how bad he was hurt until someone asked him. Amara, terrified that she'd be blamed, told him that it'd didn't hurt that much. She tried to calm him by promising him some of her candy. It didn't work. Amara always thought they were similar, but after that day, she realized that fear trumped the pain for her while pain made him forget about fear.

The three ran, Flint home where his mom would be, just getting off from work. She'd be frustrated with him for trying something so dangerous and give him a whooping. The girls ran to Ebony's house because her

dad was bedridden, so they'd be able to hide the cuts. Blood oozed from
their legs with each stride. Once at Ebony's, the girls darted to the bathroom, ripped toilet paper from the roll, knocking over the moldy plastic
cup that held toothbrushes. Her dad heard and asked from the dark bedroom what was going on.

"Everything's fine Papa," Ebony yelled. Ebony closed her bedroom
door. The girls' eyes locked and they laughed hesitantly.

"Did that just happen?" Amara asked.

"I don't even know," Ebony answered, shakily handing Amara a wet
piece of tissue. They dabbed their legs and made fans out of newspaper
to cool the cuts.

Amara wished she never let Flint onto the fence that day. She never
wanted to go on the gate again, but the pain kept bringing Flint back.
She'd find him trying to recreate the magic of the fence, but now he had
to do it alone, and it was never the same. He no longer followed Ebony
and Amara around asking to join their games. They knew where to find
him.

Ebony's dad died a month later, and a woman Amara had never seen
before came to pick Ebony up. The woman placed her hand on Ebony's
back, urging her into the black car. From her yard, Amara called over to
her and Ebony turned, put her hand up and smirked. Then she was ushered into the car. As they drove away, Amara felt the pull of Ebony
disappearing from her life. Amara blamed the gate even though deep
down she knew there were other factors at play. Factors she didn't quite
understand yet but felt their presence.

Amara tried to get Flint into other things, but he only cared for the
fence. Watching Flint attempt to recreate that day pained Amara and
one day she looked away and focused on the future. As they got older,
their differences solidified their distance. Flint still reached for that bit
of cloud, but gravity snapped him back down at a faster rate. Because of
this, his cuts were always deeper, and the scars more severe.

At family gatherings, they tell Amara she is the good twin, but she hides
the gnawing guilt that she isn't. After all, she showed the fence to Flint.
She lit the match that ignited his addiction. She ignored his late-night
calls when he needed a place to sleep and kept him away from the life

she built. A life where her daughter wore Sunday dresses that fit with shiny shoes and lacy socks. A life where no fences were needed because her property stretched for miles.

Yet she found there's something stronger than the gates she puts up. It's a bond that drills through the facades of the everyday. Something that causes her to stop whatever she is doing and know something is happening with Flint. He has the same feeling when he isn't preoccupied with the fence. In his moments of clarity, he shows up or calls right when she's amid something heavy. These diversions from reality show her what it'd be like if Flint never went on the fence.

He comes to her door, and he isn't shaking or impatient. His sentences are clear and concise, so she lets him in. Amara prepares two cups of green tea with slices of lemon and honey. She goes to the living room to see him on her couch. He's reclined, his arms spread out on the backside of the sofa, and he's admiring the lush backyard through the floor-to-ceiling windows. Amara walks up and he grabs the tea from her.

"Remember that time Mom and Dad took us to the ocean. We drove hundreds of miles, and you wouldn't even go in the damn water," Flint laughs, sinking back into the couch.

"I was fascinated and scared. I mean, by the power of it and how it came in then retreated. I didn't want to get pulled out to sea," Amara replied.

Amara later learned that blood isn't blue. Veins appear so because of the way the light hits them. But she now knows there's something in blood that causes family to be drawn together as the sea is drawn out to shore. That something has the power to permit occasions like this; moments where she can peek into another reality. This entity causes the gate to occasionally bend, and Flint and Amara can reach each other through the barricades that divide them.

Mel needs a new name

Dear Mr. Davies,

I am writing this long letter to you because this is one of the few things I am certain about. You see, I have had doubts about a lot of things. I have stood on the thin line between atheism and Sunday school, I have written a thesis I wasn't sure of, and have swallowed the pill of uncertainty life gives to all of us. So, when I tell you I am sure about this, you should pull your socks off, fold your sleeves, put on those reading glasses you use only at the office, and read this.

I am writing this because Mel needs a new name.

I am sitting at my dining table, the one with nothing that relates to food, but everything that screams books. Books on psychology, the human mind, and therapy. This paper is balanced on the scaffold of my copy of Dorian's book on psychology. I have just eaten a bowl of cold spaghetti; I had to eat it cold because I knew that if I had warmed it, the intensity with which I wrote this letter would be reduced, pulverized even. Today was the fifth therapy session with your daughter. The fifth time I have sat across from your daughter trying to reach into her soul.

All the things I have come to know about Mel are stored in an amber-colored jar in the recesses of my mind, because I want to prevent any kind of effervescence.

Can I tell you something? I used to love writing when I was younger. It started with a longing to talk to someone, anyone, about the insecurities I faced. There was no one and so I started to keep a diary. When I was a teenager, that diary was the closest thing to a video of my life. I wrote about the days when my mum left me for Kano to run her many businesses. I wrote about the uncertainties of not having a father, the struggles, the many questions that ravaged my mind. I wrote poems too. Poems of longing and sunset.

Mel reminds me of the poems I used to write. Disjointed, strewn about like the body parts of my mum as she lay dead in Kano. An arm here, a femur there, a rib forcefully jettisoned from its initial position, grotesque. Those were the saddest days of my life you know, I was burning hot with revenge for the people who had killed my mum. Those were the days I stopped writing too. A life so fickle was not worth writing about.

I remember the first time Mel walked into my office. I knew in that instant that she was unique. First, I did not have my ten minutes of clearing-my-head time; she came at exactly three p.m. I must tell you why that stood out to me.

Since I came back to Nigeria to practice after college, I have worked with a rigid routine. I get to the office by 9 a.m. I have my first session by 10 a.m., after an hour of yoga and mind prepping, till noon, after which I have a lunch break. The second patient comes in by 1 p.m. and leaves by 3 p.m. and the third comes then till 6 p.m. The patients do not come at their exact time, so I have time to clear my head. A ten-minute break cut out by the universe for me. Mel came at exactly 3 p.m. It was the second reason I doubted she was Nigerian, or even African.

Our first session was different from the usual cold, deathly stares I get from patients. I didn't expect a patient to be so chatty. Her calm was ostensible. In her flat black shoes, she walked round my office, observing, looking at pictures and the artwork at the left corner of the room. She read the *Say No to Depression* tag on the flyer pasted behind the door. She touched my flower vase and commented about the lavender's almost wilting state. She was like an owner observing her new house, savoring every moment, anticipating the memories she would make there. I watched her breathe in the air and signaled for her to sit.

"I hate sitting," she said, almost immediately.

It came as a shock, my mind was already searching for a diagnosis, physical appearance, gait, gesticulations. *Maybe she needs sedatives or she's mentally deranged or schizophrenia...no I think it's bipolar disorder, I mean she's starting to get aggressive.*

"What's your name?" I asked as soon as she leaned forward on the chair in front of her.

She didn't reply, her eyes on a picture above the mini shelf on the right. She was looking at my framed certificate.

"Where are your parents?" I asked.

"Parent," she cut in. "He's not here."

"Okay. What is your name?"

"Mel Davies."

I looked up, she was definitely Nigerian. The tan skin, kinky hair, and plump body couldn't have said otherwise.

I started to write *Melissa* before I asked what Mel meant.

"Melancholy," she said.

I was stunned. I knew Nigerians gave their children strange names. I'd heard about a couple who named their twins Trust and Obey and another couple who named their triplets Miracles, Signs, and Wonders because they were born during a church program that had the theme. But Melancholy...I had never heard that.

"I get that all the time, my name has a story." She saw my expression even without looking at me.

I wanted to hear the story but I didn't want to pry.

"You schooled in Pennsylvania? How impressive!" she said, her eyes still on the certificate. "Why did you choose to be a therapist?"

"I did not exactly choose it. I just needed to do something with my degree in psychology, and since I didn't want to teach, I decided to become a therapist."

"How old are you?" she asked.

I pause. Nobody asked their therapist these kinds of questions. "Thirty-five," I answered, cringing, for the question that always followed was the question about my husband.

"You're a Miss," she said and smiled. "I am twenty-two."

"Why do you think you need therapy?"

"There is something growing in my chest."

I stared at her with furrowed brows. I scribbled 'confused state' on the sheet. "How do you know something is growing in your chest? Should that even be true, you do not need therapy, you need a surgeon."

"It's like a tumor, it was this size before." She raised a fist. "I feel like it's going to explode any moment from now, like a tsunami."

"That still does not explain why you need therapy."

"It metastasizes, but this time, not to distant organs but to people."

The first thing you learn about therapy is the act of being calm. I tried hard to keep it in.

She smiled then, like this was a sport, reciting gibberish to therapists and watching them cringe. "In plain words, I bring bad luck."

I looked at her intensely, trying to pick out something, a peripheral inkling, something that pointed to the fact that she was out of her mind. She was calm, her eyes fixed on mine.

"What is my diagnosis and treatment?" she asked after few minutes.

I thought about what to say. There is no medical diagnosis for bringing bad luck to people.

"I am not sure," I said, honestly. "I think we need to reschedule while I do a little research about all you have told me."

She turned to leave.

"Mel? Can you call me later today?"

She turned back and looked at me with a peculiar, unreadable expression. She took my card and then opened the door to leave.

Mel did not call me.

Mister Davies, I must say, your daughter's eccentricity tugs at a person's mind. It folds itself into a slight weight that sits in your heart, runs around your floors, and stains your walls, like a two-year-old. I thought about her while I cooked my meal that night, in my car as I waited for the Apapa expressway traffic to dissipate.

One morning, a bird perched on the rail in my corridor. It was yellow. So beautiful. It stared at me right in the eye and surveyed my corridor. It saw the loneliness that plagued me, the pin-drop silence that engulfed my apartment. It flew away with all it had garnered. It would take it to its flock, chirp about a lonely, sick woman it had met. They would laugh and scorn and maybe cry for me. I wish I had someone to talk to about Mel that way except for my stucco walls and large television.

Our second session was hasty.

I was pissed at how cheery she seemed. She asked endless questions like I was a transparent wall and she could see the loneliness that had eaten deep into me. I wanted to ask about her friends, whether they gossiped about therapists with their noses stuck up in the air, feeling like they had the answers to their problems.

She came at 3 p.m. again. I had just finished a session with a boy with Obsessive-Compulsive disorder. He had begun by picking up the pens on the floor and shifting my books, like something in his mind screamed 'clean, clean, clean!' I allowed him do his bits and prescribed a refill of the same pills for him. It was obvious he had been skipping his pills.

Again, I didn't have an answer to Mel's problem. Her session was last, and so I carried her with me as I walked the lone street to my apartment, thinking about how not-in-need-of-therapy she seemed.

I went home that night to find her on social media. Her Instagram account was private and I couldn't risk giving her the impression that I was stalking her. The headlines would read: *Therapist is a serial stalker* and a lot of people would even read 'serial killer.' I put down my phone in frustration.

Our third session was the beginning of an unplanned friendship.

"Why do you think people arrive late for events and hide their lack of punctuality under the shadow of 'African time'?" she asked.

"I think it's because they know that those events will not start on time." That was the only logical answer I could give.

"So what happened to waiting till the event starts? What happened to putting your thoughts together and surveying the environment and taking in deep breaths?" She brought out a pink big journal, one she scribbled things on as we talked, the one I yearned to read. "I have a theory about African time," she said and chuckled. "People love African time because they are afraid. They are afraid of being alone. The event organizers are afraid of conducting an event for only themselves and the guests are afraid of staying alone. It's a kind of phobia. I will look it up and tell you during our next session."

Mel's mind is a mine, unreachable and untamable.

"What phobias do you have?"

"I fear water."

"Why?"

"Something so free has got some nerve, it reminds me of something I can never be."

On the days before our session, I walk around with my mind in my hands. I flip and flip, through memories of past therapies, classes I took while in college. Looking for something, anything that would click, anything that could lead me to the solution to Mel's problems. Anything that could maybe sate her for a while, giving me time to refer her to somebody else. Nothing made sense, depression or bipolar disorder didn't cut it. I must confess, she made me read a lot, she made me search for answers in mundane things, in everyday events, in people's eyes.

I guess that's what happens when a person gives themself over to you. You are engulfed by their identity so much so that it is intertwined with your own. Therapy is the result of empathy after all. But this, this is not empathy at all. It is a kind of intersection I cannot quite explain.

It was during our third session that she told me about you. It was a fluid conversation that somehow had you as the epicenter.

"Are you happy?" I asked.

"What does that mean?"

"You don't understand the word?"

"Abstract nouns are variable, I don't know how you define happiness."

"Okay, are you sad?"

"I don't know either."

"How do you feel then?"

"I feel like my life is moving slower than I am."

"How?"

"It feels like I'm putting on a magnifying lens. Every detail is intensified, every experience is imprinted in my mind like an office stamp."

"So you remember all experiences clearly?" This was my chance. "Do you mind talking about some of them?"

"I miss my Dad," she said after a pause that seemed like forever.

"Where is he?"

"I don't know. He's like water."

"You don't live with him?"

"I live alone. He lives with his new wife."

"What about your mum?"

"She's gone. She died as soon as I was born."

"Oh my, I'm sorry."

"My name is Melancholy because that's how my dad felt after I was born."

I did not believe that at all. She talked about you. You used to love her in bits. In small portions. A love that was short-changed by grief and anger. Sometimes when you were on a high, you showered on her all the leftover love from your dead wife. When you were pissed, she was a distraction. You would stare at her as she tried hard to get your attention after you came home from a long day at work. In your relationship with her, she was a shadow, a docile receptor of whatever you gave to her.

Her days at Federal Government college Ojota were a phase that led her to the realization of this deadly thing she spreads to people. The days when she sought love in the arms of naive Jss3 classmates that hedged her in, gave her a place to be. The day when they read Tim LaHaye's *Why You Act The Way You Do.*

That day, everyone had screamed, "Melancholy is sanguine," and laughed. She retreated into her shell, a carved-out safe space in her mind. There, she was not Mel the San. She was a seven-year-old princess, laughing through the darkness of the world, playing with sand houses and building blocks. She walked around in that shell from then on and that was when the tumor started to grow.

Ekanem, Mel's best friend, committed suicide.

It was during one of the school's inter-house sports competitions. All students were to go to the sports field. The teachers had come to the hostels with long canes and chased the students to the field. Mel was in SS1 then. Mr. Ajayi, the senior Physical Education teacher, was in charge of the training. They marched out in single file to the field and their names were called out in alphabetical order. When he got to Ekanem's name, no one knew where she was, including Mel. Mr. Ajayi sent Mel and other students back to the hostel to search for her. They got to her room and the sight sent screams ringing through the entire school.

They found Ekanem on the floor, a bottle of tablets emptied by her side. She was rushed to the school clinic, and there she had a cardiac arrest and died. Everyone looked at Mel with disdain How could a person be best friends with someone else and not know they were at the brink of darkness. Weren't friends supposed to share burdens, encourage each other, and dispel sadness?

Mel cried herself to sleep every night. If only the tears could wash with them the images of Ekanem's splayed limbs and the bottle of tablets.

When Mel told this story, we were sitting on the reclining chair on the balcony of my apartment. The sky was a bright blue and the world was quiet except for crickets and owls. She had come to visit me for the first time and we started talking about a lot of things. I told her about my mother, her horrific death, and she listened intently. Her eyes shone with tears, the wind carried my voice high and low. First a crescendo and then a diminuendo, like the high-pitched sopranos that sang in the choir in the Anglican church I attended as a child.

When she finished her story, it was dark. The blue clouds had gone to sleep and in their place, a gray blanket littered with a gazillion tiny stars and the half-moon casting a shadow of two women sitting side by side, crying.

We stayed that way for almost an hour before I took her into the sitting room. We slept on the couch, each rocked to sleep by our own demons, by the memories we tried to forget.

During our fourth session, she told me why she had gone to a lot of therapists since she was nineteen. It began after her breakup with Dare, her first boyfriend. They had dated for one year and it ended with Dare's mother visiting her hostel during her second year at the University of Lagos. Dare's mother was sophisticated, but the fetters of stereotype and religious superstitions still held her bound. She went to warn Mel to stay away from her son.

"A child who kills her mother and friends should not be married," she said.

Dare came later, as if cast under his mother's spell. He told her he'd heard a lot of rumors about her. That she killed Ekanem. Mr. Pelumi, the copper who was close to her, was accused of raping students and sacked. She had destroyed her roommate's relationship with her evil charm. She. Was. Evil. Dare was hurt that he heard all of this from outsiders and not from her. He was sorry but he could not continue the relationship.

She went home that night to an empty house. You were not there. She stayed outside and shed silent tears.

After the breakup, she gave it a lot of thought. She started with Google and discovered that it had no answers for a person in need of redemption. After a long search, she came across tumors in a medical journal she picked up while waiting to see the third therapist she consulted. It said tumors were neoplastic cells that had lost their apoptotic abilities and now multiplied, unregulated. She was immediately interested. She read about benign and malignant tumors. Malignant tumors were the ones that metastasized to distant organs and caused death faster. She read about women with breast cancers and mastectomy.

That night, she examined her breasts, in quadrants, as the journal had said. She checked for lumps, anything that proved she had a tumor. She stopped when there was nothing. But this was the only explanation for the symptoms she had, the fact that anyone who as much as looked at her twice was going to be knocked down by a drunk driver the next second. She repelled people, she was tired of running from the things that haunted her. It was easier to stay alone. She was not afraid to be alone anymore. That way, she was safe.

Her therapist obsession began as a need. A need to talk, to be friends with someone who was not exactly a friend. She read that tumors only spread to organs that were in a person's body, that is, her friends, people she had given her tumor-ridden heart to. Seeing therapists was a way to outsmart the tumor. She could talk, visit, and spend time with people who were not her friends. The tumor would not spread to them.

Today, during our fifth session, I called her Melancholy instead of Mel. I saw a cursory cringe, a sadness that engulfed her as soon as I said the name, like a being that had exacted its presence in our midst. It came with silence.

I stared at her, how different she looked from the girl that walked into my office at exactly 3 p.m. The girl who was not afraid of being alone. She looked small, defeated, docile. And that was when I found it. What I had been looking for all along.

My diagnosis after five sessions: Mel needs a new name.

A name is inhaled like the hot balm my mum used to massage when I had dislocated a joint as a child. A name tethers a person to the place where it was first uttered. It invokes a presence, just like the one at the office today. It takes a person and makes that person something big, bigger than the person's will. It has a mind of its own and breathes on its own.

This letter holds the sacred parts of your daughter. It's funny how you can get so involved in a person's life, live it in yourself, walk through their memories, see their fears, and match their life to yours.

I write this letter because, sometimes I am Mel, bound by the demons of my past and choked by loneliness. I write because, if a person comes to you seeking redemption, you have to save yourself first and then bring them to a place where what they seek is a river. They can drink to their fill and even have their bath and create a home with the foundations.

The world needs a new Mel, one who is afraid to be alone, arrives late for events, and makes friends, and satisfies the sanguine fire that burns inside of her. Mel needs a new name.

I hope this letter meets you well, I hope you shed tears for your little girl. I hope you carry her on your shoulders until she learns that her life is hers to have and own and live.

Love,
Miss Okorie, Mel's Therapist

Too Much of Anything Can Kill You

I lost my keys again. Mama's gonna have a fit. When Daddy was alive, losing my keys wasn't that big of a deal cause Daddy worked at the hardware store down the road and they'd just give us a new one for cheap. But Daddy died over two months ago. Him, Uncle Tim, and Sadie's dad died in a car accident. You know the kind that takes a while to identify the bodies.

I took my time walking to the house from school. Didn't wanna hear Mama's mouth about how I was too big to keep losing keys. I finally got to the house and knocked a few times, but Mama didn't answer. So, I tried my luck at turning the knob and to my surprise, the door was unlocked.

In the Spring, I don't even take my keys to school with me cause Mama leaves the door open to let fresh air in. But it's winter now so we gotta keep in all the heat we can. When I walked into the house, it was a bit warmer than usual, like Mama let the wood burn all day. She usually don't let the wood burn during the day cause we need the heat more at night. You know when the temperature is real low and the wind gets violent. And plus, that wood is just so darn heavy. When Daddy was here, he'd always give me the lightest piece to carry.

My best friend Sadie is going to be living with us soon cause her Mama died last week. I remember Tuesday night when Mama got the news. The phone rang and we happened to pick up the phone at the same time. Aunt Alice was crying on the other end so I stayed quiet to see what was wrong. Sadie's mama died of what they call an overdose last week. Mama says an overdose is when you take too much of a good thing and too much of anything can kill you.

After I overheard the news that Sadie's mama died, I hung up the phone real quick and played sleep. I knew Mama was gone come in my room to tell me and I wouldn't be able to explain why I was already crying. She knocked on the door once and lightly pushed it open.

"Sadie, you up sweetie?" she said, trying to mask the crack in her voice.

I didn't budge. I knew she would tell me in the morning. This would give me time to chew on what I just heard on the phone. And anyway, bad news is better to digest at night. The dark gives it time to settle.

The next morning when Mama told me the news, I chewed on the inside of my cheek for a bit and avoided eye contact with Mama. I tried to focus real hard on something on the kitchen table. I noticed Mama ain't been cleanin up after herself. Leaving trails of sugar or salt or something on the table all the time.

We buried Sadie's mama in the cemetery by the school a week after she died. Graveside service, quick, easy, and sad. That Wednesday, Sadie moved in. Mama figured it'd be easier to let her stay with us till the school year was over. Kinda nice having your best friend live with you. I thought it would be hard. Thought she'd be too sad to still share her secrets and sneak to put on red lipstick on Saturdays when our mamas wasn't lookin. Losing both of your parents in two months has to be hard. But she's holding up pretty well. She had a strong mama and a real tough daddy. She must've absorbed all their strength when they left. She was doing mighty fine.

After dinner every night, Mama makes us sweep the floor and wipe off the table. I know I wiped the table off last night but there's sugar all over the table this morning. Mama must of had some more rice after we all went to bed. She's the only one that puts sugar on her rice.

My parents were never the type to tell me to leave the room when company came over but every time my Aunt Alice stopped by the house, we had to go play. I'm twelve now, I don't really play that much anymore. It seems like every time Aunt Alice comes over, the sugar crumbs come with her. I was getting used to Mama making a mess all over the house. It seems like every time I cleaned some up, it came up somewhere else.

And Mama ain't found a job since Daddy died, so she and Aunt Alice spend a whole lot of time at the kitchen table. There must be something really good at that table. Every time Mama and Aunt Alice leave the table there's a real distant look in their eyes. Like they in the clouds or somethin.

Everything has been different since Daddy died. Mama's surviving but I don't think she's livin much. And she's getting real skinny now like she don't spend all her time at that table. I know for a fact she's eatin good. I just don't know what it is that's filling her up. I'm starting to get worried bout mama. She looking real tiny and Aunt Alice seems to always be sleep on the couch.

Spring is here now and school is almost out. I can't wait to visit Grandma this summer. People are starting to talk. My teacher say she ain't seen Mama at church in a while and the neighbors keep saying "God bless yo mama, Sadie."

Daddy died a while ago, I figured the prayers would of stopped weeks ago.

Well, I made an A on my math test. I'd been working hard to get them numbers right. I walked real fast home to show Mama but she wasn't there when I got there. The lady next door, Ruby, said Mama went away for a while so me and Sadie gotta stay with her until school let out, and then I was gonna go stay with Grandma for the summer and Sadie was gone go live with an aunt up north. She didn't bother to tell me where Mama went. It ain't like her to just up and leave without tellin me.

I left my math test on the table so it could be the first thing Mama see when she got back. Once I stuffed my suitcase with all my favorite clothes, I headed out the door over to Ruby. I noticed some more of that sugar or salt on the table and decided to clean it up before I left. Mama say it's bad luck to come back to a dirty home.

Ruby drove me to Bama in her two-door hot box. We call it a hot box cause she ain't got no air in it. Got to ride with the windows down and pray it don't rain. Whole time down, I wanted to ask when Mama would be back, but I decided not to.

Well, Grandma still looks the same. Seventy going on thirty-five. Her hair is all the way grey now though, not just sprinkled grey like the last time I seen her. We talked about school and boys and Mama.

This summer at Grandma's has been a real funny one. And I don't mean funny like I'm laughing all the time, I mean funny like it feels different. Everyone is always asking me how I'm holding up but I'm not sure what I need holding up for. I mean, I ain't seen or talked to Mama, but I know she'll be back pretty soon. When Grandpa died when I was real little, she had to go away for a while too. I know she'll be back.

Grandma is getting more visitors than usual and I always hear them talking about how hard it must be to take a child in at her age, but I visit Grandma's every summer and that's never been the topic.

Any other summer it's, "How you been?" or "You enjoying yaself back here in these woods?"

I was always told to stay out of grown folks' business, but I keep overhearing my name in conversations. I try real hard not to listen but I just can't help myself. I keep hearing the word *user* over and over again. I tried to look it up in the book of words but...none of the explanations made sense.

One night I went to the kitchen for a glass of water. This south Georgia heat shole can leave your throat dry. On my way to the kitchen, I overheard Grandma and her neighbor Ms. Ann talking.

"How long you think she gone be gone?" Ms. Ann asked.

"I don't know. I don't understand how she got this way. Death can do some strange things to you. When Rufus died, I didn't become no user, never even thought about it," Grandma said.

"Well everybody ain't strong you know? You just gotta keep prayin. Pray until you can't pray no more," Ms. Ann said.

All of a sudden my throat wasn't dry no more. I went back to my room to get some rest.

One morning, Grandma made a big breakfast. You know the kind with all the fixins. Sausage. Grits. Eggs. Pancakes. I only get this kind of breakfast when I first get here and when I'm leaving to go back to Georgia.

In the middle of breakfast Grandma say, "Sadie, I think you're old enough to hear this now. Ya mama been sick since ya daddy died."

"Is it the sugar or maybe the salt?" I ask.

"The sugar or salt?" she responded.

"Yeah, Mama been eating a bunch of sugar or salt or something since Daddy died. I always have to clean it up. It be everywhere Grandma. When her appetite changed, she changed too," I said.

Grandma just stared at me for a while and then told me to finish my plate.

Later that summer Grandma tells me that Mama is a user and that she could've ended up like Sadie's mama if she didn't get some help. I'm still not sure what a user is but for the rest of the summer, I made sure Grandma didn't salt them greens like crazy or add sugar to her rice. I didn't wanna to lose her too.

Spirit Week

I heard about Erika Ball during Spirit Week, my first Spirit Week of middle school. From underneath the beanie that Momma let me borrow for Hat Day, I watched a few eighth-grade boys as they said, "No bro, she fell from the top floor. Out of the window."

"Who?"

"Erika."

"Erika Ball?"

"Erika's got balls."

They laughed as if they were friendly, but when their eyes noticed that I was staring, that I was holding the food in my mouth still so it wouldn't hinder my listening, they shot side-eyes at one another and I knew to look away.

"You're scaring the kids," one of them joked.

"You're scaring me!" another shouted. "I don't wanna see a girl with balls."

They erupted in laughter, spraying bits of Frosted Flakes across the cafeteria table like confetti.

After my fifth-grade graduation ceremony, there was no need to ask what was next. When my class walked into the gymnasium, we were met with our families, all standing and clapping as we walked through and onto the makeshift stage, marked off as a rectangle of blue painter's tape on the floor. As a kid in Rockwell, you dreamed of that moment. The moment where you would move up to Langford Middle School and be with the big kids.

Langford was the only middle school in Rockwell, so unless Momma and Dad wanted to move, there was no other choice. But it was a good choice and I already knew all about the building. Langford had three floors and a basement. Eighth grade on the third floor. Seventh grade on the second, with the music classrooms. And sixth grade shared the first floor with the cafeteria and the gymnasium with the real bleachers and the famous girl's locker room, the one that's haunted.

"No, like it's definitely haunted," Avery said during the first week of school.

"How do you know?"

"Because I've tried it already! You turn off the lights, look into the full body mirror, and say Bloody Mary three times."

"Oh my God, you saw her?" I gasped.

"Well no, not actually. I said her name once and then stopped. But I know it's real! I've heard other people talk about it too."

Avery said it like it was fact. Like it wasn't anything different than what any teacher has said.

There are seven continents. The mitochondria is the powerhouse of the cell. Langford's girl's locker room is haunted.

"Maybe it's haunted by Erika..." I looked away as I said it, waiting for Avery to beg me to tell her more.

"Who is Erika?"

I didn't know Erika. And I didn't want to. Imagining her as my reflection was scary enough. Or what if it was during science class, when I asked to use the restroom right before it was time to popcorn read from the textbook. Erika would meet me, each of us standing and staring from either end of the fifth-grade hall, shards of glass pierced through her clothing. Or maybe she'd wait until I was in the stall, sitting on a silent toilet, staring at the back of the door that read things like: "Ms. Smith iz gay" and "MJ+RC=LUV." Erika, with grass plastered to the dried spit around her mouth, would appear headfirst underneath the stall.

"She's an eighth-grader. I guess she just fell out of a window here. She bounced like a ball...or something," I explained.

"Did she jump out?"

I never held eye contact for so long, my words sweetly resting in my mouth, both of our swelling chests folding over our lunch trays as we inched closer to one another over the cafeteria table.

"I don't know," I finally whispered, trying desperately to keep a secret that the whole school already knew. And no one around us cared anyway. No one could hear us, pushed away in a corner of the room. Most of the time, no one even saw us.

Friday was pajama day. Avery wore a purple Bobby Jack set. The smiling monkey printed all over her shirt matched the monkey stuffed animal that she kept in the middle of her bed. During our sleepovers, she never found it funny when I snatched the stuffed animal and ran around the house with it, Avery running right behind me. It always ended in us getting yelled at and Avery tucking the monkey back into her bed, as careful as she could.

Before school on Friday, Momma found me in our laundry room, which was just our basement, reaching waist-deep in a hamper full of dirty clothes. In the couple of years that we lived in that place, we always joked about how creepy the basement was, as a way to make us feel better about going down there. So, when I ducked my head low, cautious of a swooping bat, I could laugh about how I looked like a scuttling crab. Or when a sock slipped from the basket of laundry when walking up the basement stairs, we decided that it vanished off into a portal, rather than looking for it and finding who knows what.

"Aye, we gotta go," Momma called, hunched over on the staircase. "What are you doing?"

Holding the only pair of pajama pants I owned, the red plaid ones that sat an inch higher than the average highwater, she put the picture together quickly.

"No, you aren't wearing those. I can smell those from here. That's why I told you to put those in the wash last night."

"We should check it out," Avery suggested.

"What?" I slammed my milk down on my tray, dramatically, because it felt appropriate.

"You can but I'm not."

"Come on. We'll go together, really quick."

"How can we go together?" I asked.

"During lunch on Monday. You ask Mrs. Jones to go to the bathroom and I'll ask Ms. Smith." She shrugged like she had the plan thought out already.

"Why do you want to go so bad?" fear of the reality suddenly in my voice.

"Because," Avery groaned, "there's no way the story is true. We'll just walk past the classrooms, see if there are any broken windows, then leave. Easy."

"Easy," I repeated.

"Five more minutes, fifth grade!" Mrs. Jones called out. "Five minutes!"

The two of us looked down at our trays.

"I'm not really hungry anymore," I said.

"I am," Avery laughed, her mouth already full of Mexican pizza.

I used my spork to make quick designs in my corn and then watched it slowly seep back into the shape of the square it sat in.

Our plan wouldn't have been the first time I lied to a teacher.

It started the year before, every week or so, about three minutes after returning from recess. I'd stand from my seat, walk over to the teacher who was preparing her textbook and worksheets for Language Arts when I'd whisper shyly, directly to her stomach and then walk straight out the door. A hush of "Where is she going?" filled the room as I tried not to make eye contact with anyone because I knew all eyes were on me. I felt cool getting to leave the room. Getting to skip a couple minutes of the lesson. I felt good. Who else could just get up and leave like that?

I'd walk down to the front office, watching as the secretary filed through the drawer of inhalers, all with different names P̲ost-it noted to them. I'd take two long puffs of mine, even though I wasn't wheezing.

"On your way back to class, stop and get a little water, sweetie."

And I would. Taking my time, acting like I was still catching my breath, like I had just run a mile, if anyone else passed me in the hall.

But at Langford, there weren't recesses. There was gym class, still, but if I complained of my asthma to Mr. Poole, he'd tell me that I needed to bring my inhaler to class or leave a spare in the locker room.

I had to find a new way to get attention. A new way to be cool.

I wanted the weekend to exhaust the myth. I hoped that by Monday, Avery forgot about Erika. Or that Erika would've just walked home and that the window, wherever it was, would be completely repaired. Instead, on Monday, during lunch, Avery and I climbed the stairs up to the third floor. And instead of looking cool, I froze and shushed Avery at any slight sound.

"We have to be fast," Avery whispered.

"I don't even know where we're going," I replied. "It could've been any of these classrooms."

We walked past the doors, scanning each classroom as much as we could. Without really looking, I felt hundreds of eyes shooting up at me in the flash that I walked by a class, then heard laughter echoing in each of my steps.

"I think my brother had this teacher," Avery said, huddled down in a door frame.

"I don't see anything, let's just go."

There were footsteps behind us, kicking across the carpet with each stride. I stopped, ready to turn around and apologize for lying, apologize for being in the wrong place, apologize to Erika that I ever questioned if she were real. And Avery stood, walked down the hall without me, determined to get away.

"I didn't know it was crazy hair day," a voice behind me cackled.

I turned and saw three girls, with their three pointer fingers in my face.

On Monday, everyone wore their favorite color. I felt like I fit in with all of the other girls who I knew would wear pink, and I knew I'd have to go into my older sister's closet. On Tuesday, when I wore one of my dad's basketball jerseys as a dress, no one even noticed. On Wednesday, mismatch day, when the patterns of my clothes screamed out loud, no one batted an eye. Thursday, everyone's faces were hidden under funny hats. And on Friday, I told anyone who asked me that I actually was wearing my pajamas. That I slept in jeans all the time.

And then we all went back to normal.

There were three girls standing in front of me, teasing me, because on that day of the week, I looked like myself.

"How does she even get it like that?" one of the girls asked, her eyes locked on the top of my head, her finger doing swirls or question marks in the air.

"Does she own a brush? They aren't that expensive," the girl with skin like salmon said, turning her words to me.

I felt my hair crawl on my head like worms growing from my scalp. I turned to look for Avery, praying that she was there waiting for me, motioning her hands at me, saying "Come on! Come on!" But she was gone. As the tears formed in my eyes, I hoped that I'd at least get to see Erika, covered in blood, limping toward me, making the gang of three girls shriek and run away. "This school is so gross!" they'd scream.

It took a week for things to die down, for Langford to move onto something new, to start hearing new things in the cafeteria over breakfast.

Savannah Stewart had sex with a dog. Ava and Christine fought during lunch and it lasted the whole period. I heard they took breaks in between punches to take bites of their pizza. Dominique slapped Marco in the face. (It's crazy because Marco took karate classes). Reggie got a video of the whole fight on his phone.

ADRIAN JOSEPH

Free Falling

I don't know what made me agree to this exercise, but here I am. All 5 feet and 120 pounds of me, walking slowly down a flickering hallway which seems to stretch into forever. This is the heaviest I've ever felt. Despite my size, I am an ocean. A body of sorrow. Chest filled with secrets that could swallow down a whole kingdom.

My heart is eager to begin, but my feet, they drag as if I have been walking dead. Tangled in a grim reaper lineage, leading me to my grave. I want to tell her a bad feeling lives inside my bones. I want to say, *Let's go back the way we came*, but Hope, the "resolutionist," walks on my left, insisting that this is a sure-fire way to gain closure from all I've been through.

"I've done it myself," she tells me with brightness in her voice.

I can't remember the last time my voice was bright. There is no light in it. Just a hollow space for words to stumble through whenever I say the things I won't regret, instead of the things I need to say. Nobody listens much anyway. Which makes Hope an angel of sorts.

We met at city park. I was ashamed to tell her I'd been sleeping there, so I did not. I watched her run so many laps that I felt tired myself. I saw my life in all her sweat. Dripping down into the blacktop, no match for the light of day, dissolving back into the nothingness from which it came. When she asked my name, I literally told her, "I am nothing."

She told me there's a secret place for girls who are named Nothing. A special place for girls like me who say very little but think a whole lot of things, and I suppose, I can't remember the last time I had a place to belong. A reservation.

The trees have been my sanctuary. The birds, the bees, my therapists. They know my story. To the town that chewed me up and spit me out, mine is not special in the least.

Hope smiled and begged to differ. Her smile, unique. Sweet, deep and bright like ripened tangerines.

When we approach a wide steel door. Hope stands in front of me. She hands me a small strip of paper and tells me to place it beneath my tongue where it will dissolve. I hesitate but she reassures me by looking deep into my eyes.

"This is it. Behind this door is everything. Only one way in and one way out, so once I close it there is no going back. Considering that, I have to ask you once again, are you truly ready to let go of whatever hurt you?"

My hands are sweaty. I want to run away, but running is all I've done for years. And if she's right, if this place will help me to finally put the past behind me, then what is there left for me to lose? Pushing a loose curl behind my ear, I take a deep breath, then nod my head.

Hope flashes a warm smile and grabs me by both my shaking shoulders.

"You'll be fine. I promise. This is just the last stop before you move into a brand-new life."

I search her face for sincerity. Her eyes are filled to the brim with the stuff.

When she slides the door open, I brace myself for monsters of every kind to reach out and grab me, but nothing happens. I peer in as far as I can but there is no sign of movement, no sign of life. Is it a grave?

Glancing, confused, I make a face.

She urges me on.

"Your fear is the anchor. Remember the mantras I taught you?" she quizzes.

I say aloud into the darkness, "I hold the light. I hold the answers. I am the truth."

Stepping into it, I pray I am no fool for trusting her.

Hope chimes in, "Keep moving forward." Then softly closes the door behind me.

Obscurity welcomes me into its belly with one huge gulp. The high-pitched tone of silence finds its way into my ears, its frequency maddening. I chant my mantras one after the other until I make some sort of tangible peace with wherever I stand.

I can't see anything. Extending both my arms in front of me, I begin to feel my way through the room, one step at a time.

"Keep moving forward. Keep moving forward. You can do this. Keep moving forward." I encourage myself.

I'm not sure how long it takes my hands to stiffen against cool, textured hardness, but eventually, they do. I am frisking a wall, patting it down like it's a criminal in possession of an exit sign, but there is nothing. Trying not to panic, I use it as a guide. Slowly scaling horizontally until alas, there is a break inside the structure.

My mind wanders to what got me here, shuffling through a collection of faces before landing on the one which nearly haunted me to suicide. I close my eyes and it makes no difference. His crooked mouth taunts with all the things wicked people say.

"You'll never get out Nia. You belong to the night."

His voice is loud and close, as if he's been in here waiting for me. It crackles in a sinister way, full of rasp from years of argument and smoking. Tobacco coats his jagged breath. I recall stained teeth and dingy gums. His ugly smile poking at me. This can't be real.

"Go away," I whisper.

"You know, you were born to be sold and bought. Sold and bought. Over and over...just like your mama." He wheezes the words and they sting my brain.

"Go away!" I demand. Louder this time.

I fight off tears and slowly turn to see him face to face. When I do, the memories come rushing back. I see the man who tried to sell me. Red as my own flesh and blood, my own grandfather.

"You're dead. You're dead." I close my eyes tight.

He cackles obnoxiously.

"Aww baby girl, you know people like me don't die. No time for reunions. I've got three Johns lined up and ready to pay, so quit playing around and get your ass back home!"

"No! You don't own me. I'm not a little girl anymore!" My voice is loud enough to fill the room. I am an ocean.

"You'll always be my little girl," he reminisces. "Mine by the blood. In fact, you'll be whatever I tell you to be. Now get on your knees and pray to God before God gets angry."

He fumbles with something and then I hear his pants unzip.

"Let me help you," he laughs. "Thy rod and thy staff, they comfort me...say it!"

Remembering the break in the wall, I slow my breath. I hold the light. I hold the answers. With my hands, I give him nothing.

Before he can say another word, I force my body to move but the next step forward causes my heart to sink down into my shoes.

There is no floor on the other side. I am falling. Falling fast through all the darkness and into the deep. I fall away from him and allow him to fall away from me. The sound is reminiscent of Velcro ripping. The feeling, next of kin to death and all that death brings. Joy and mourning. Life and possibility. I fall for all eternity. For every Black girl who's cried for help in the darkness and had to respond to herself. I fall, for every woman who's said, "No," only to have bad things happen anyway. I fall for forever. I fall for Hope. I fall for my mother. I fall until I realize falling is not something my kind can do. I understand, I am flying.

Then, the wind is knocked right out of me. My heart beats quickly inside my throat, a rush of life I do not recognize. I let it settle in as I entertain the thought that perhaps I have shattered into a thousand tiny pieces at the bottom of a well. I don't know what to make of myself anymore, but this I know, I am no longer tied to him. I am light.

When that relief enters my body, I feel a net beneath my legs and back. The hands that catch me, swaddling my body as if I have been newly born. My eyes adjusting, I see the glow of an exit sign.

Tilting my head, thin slivers of light break through the deep and release from mother net's gossamer grip.

Hope's voice shaves off the silence. It holds a smile, offering it to me.

"Hi. My name is Hope. What's yours?"

I think about the question for a while before exhaling.

"I am free."

Salvation

I was seven when Momma had me baptized. Momma, me, Duey, the preacher, and the church went down to the river to do it.

It was a Saturday. The river was too far away from the church to make it a part of regular service. After, there was gonna be a celebration. We all drove our cars and parked on the side of the hill that separated us from the river.

I didn't know how to swim and being in water scared me. Momma said the preacher wouldn't let me drown because Jesus was with me.

Thou I walk through the valley of the shadow of death.

We walked up the hill and through a trail in the tall grass singing church hymns and old spirituals. I was too nervous to sing.

Hold to God's unchanging hand.

Momma said I had to wear all white like a bride, only my dress was plain. It hung off my body like it didn't care that I was wearing it. I was young, and there was nothing for the dress to hold to anyway.

Seek to gain the Heavenly treasures
They will never pass away.

Momma wrapped my hair up in a white turban to match my white dress. It was tight around my head and squeezed my temples. I told her I didn't want to wear it. She told me to hush.

God's unchanging hand.

I stood in line to be baptized. There were five of us, and I was the youngest. I looked for Momma, but I couldn't see her. I watched as the pastor led the man in front of me out into the river.

The river wasn't still like I thought. It moved and swirled as it caught itself around the bodies of the preacher and the man. The preacher put one arm behind the man's back and made him cross his hands over his chest. The preacher held up his other hand and called out to us.

"This man has given himself to the Lord God and Jesus Christ, Almighty."

The congregation murmured their amens and yes Lords.

I didn't say anything.

"I Baptize you in the name of the Father, the Son, and the Holy Ghost. The preacher lowered the hand he had held up in the sky and placed it over the man's eyes. He leaned in close and pushed his body back, bending it into the water. When the man reappeared, he was in shock. The pastor needed help to steady him. When he was steady, he looked different. Like he had seen another world. When the man was out of the water, the preacher offered his hand to me.

Build your hopes on things eternal
Hold to God's unchanging hand
Trust in Him who will not leave you.

I didn't go at first. I had to make my feet move. When I stepped into the river, I could feel the cold water on my feet. The water got hold of my clothes and started rising up like it wanted to pull me in. One of the ministers had to help me. He grabbed me and guided me through the water to where the preacher was.

There was so much water. It was growing on me. The water grew up my skirt like little hands sliding over my body tryna pull me under. The water slid over my stomach and stretched up my chest. It smelled like wet dirt.

The minister had to hold me up. I couldn't feel the bottom of the river. I kept thinking about what Momma told me. Jesus.

He may not come when you want him
Hold to God's unchanging hand.

The preacher whispered something in my ear, and that's when I heard him. Jesus came to me right then. I closed my eyes and crossed my hands over my chest. The preacher raised his hand to the congregation. He called to them, but I couldn't hear it. I closed my eyes. There was a voice. "I Jesus Christ in the name of the father..."

I felt myself falling backward. The water was all around me. It was in my nose and my ears. I could see tiny bubbles and the sun. I saw it shining through the ripples of the water.

***

Being alone used to bother me. Now that I've been baptized, I don't mind it so much. I look forward to it. I like to listen to the stillness. I know that in the stillness I can hear the voice of God whispering to me.

I used to sit in my closet and read the Bible because whenever David prayed to God, he did it alone. That's what I learned in Bible school. One time, Duey found me and hollered at Momma that I was pretending to be a pair of shoes. He doesn't understand.

When we were kids, Duey used to tease me and say I need a man. I'd tell him no. I need Jesus. Momma thought that was funny, but I was serious.

The Bible says study and show yourself worthy.

***

Jimmy Davis had been watching me for weeks. If I ever forgot, Duey made it a point to remind me.

"What about Jimmy?" Duey asked. Duey's head looked like a box that got wet, and when it was hung out to dry, it stretched into a rectangle. All the girls thought he was cute.

"I dunno."

"Well he likes you," Duey said, wearing a sly grin.

"That's fine," I said, trying to let Duey know he wasn't gonna bother me.

"Duey leave your sister alone," Momma said. She was still wearing her pink satin night bonnet and her cheetah print nightgown. Duey was still smiling.

"He wants to know if he can take you out," he said.

I could feel my face heating up. I tried not to smile, but I knew Duey could see it coming.

"Oh, so you do like him," he said.

I didn't say anything back. I kept eating my breakfast and avoiding him. Duey took this as a sign to keep teasing me.

"That's too bad," he said, shaking his head slowly like he was disappointed. "He told me he really wanted to take you out."

I cut him a look. "Momma!"

"Duey stop now. Leave your sister alone," Momma said, popping him with the dry dish rag.

"I'm just playing Momma," Duey said, laughing as he ducked.

"You better get ready to go to work. I know that much," Momma said, and Duey got up from the table laughing.

When Duey was gone, she turned to me. "So..."

I looked up at her. She sat down on the chair across from me. She was smiling, but I could tell she was tired. She looked like her soul woke up before her body was ready.

***

Jimmy took me to the boardwalk for our first date. He was tall and slim. He had smooth brown skin that reflected the light of the moon. I wore a yellow collared shirt with a white skirt. Jimmy couldn't take his eyes off me. We walked and talked, and he bought me ice cream. Jimmy took me to walk on the beach, and as we walked, the tide took our footprints away. I told him about how I was afraid of the water. He laughed and told me that he would protect me. When the wave rolled in, he splashed me.

He took me under the pier. I didn't want to go. He started touching me and telling me things.

Our Father who art in heaven.

We took off our shoes. I could feel the wet sand beneath my feet. Jimmy left our shoes somewhere; I don't remember where he put them. Somewhere safe. Whenever the waves rolled in, I could feel the water wrapping itself around my feet.

Forgive us this day our trespasses.

I could feel his hands moving up my legs as the water rushed around my ankles.

As we forgive those who trespass against us.

Behind him, I could see the moon bobbing on the surface of the water.

Lead us not into temptation.

He laid me down in the dunes and caressed my hair gently.

Deliver us from evil.

I felt his hands move over my body.

For thine is the kingdom.

I closed my eyes.

The power and glory.

He told me I had to be quiet.

Forever and ever.

Amen.

***

I don't feel whole anymore. When I go into the closet to pray, I don't hear God anymore. I hear someone else.

This voice is different.

I imagine my life without the voice because now I don't hear it in silence anymore. It comes to me at the dinner table or when I'm walking down the street. I tell it to go away, but it keeps coming back.

I don't feel like it's God.

***

My stomach woke me up. The room was dark, and when I reached for Jimmy, he wasn't there. All I could feel was the pain in my stomach. I had to hold myself. The part of my nightshirt was warm and sticky. I rolled over and reached for the light on my nightstand. I was laying in blood. My blood. Something inside me felt like crying. I wanted to scream but I couldn't. I closed my eyes and tried to pray, but I couldn't.

I sat in silence in my blood, the blood of my baby.

Whiter than the snow.

I got out of bed.

Grievous were the sorrows He bore.

I walked to the bathroom. I could feel the blood between my legs.

May I to that fountain be led.

I got in the tub and turned on the faucet. I let the bathtub fill up with water.

Father, I have wandered from Thee.

Father, I have wandered from Thee.

Father, I have wandered from Thee.

The water came to my feet, and I could feel it on my back. It rose past my feet and up my thighs. It rose up my nightshirt. All the water took the color of my blood.

Crimson do my sins seem to me.

I cupped my hands together and lifted them out of the water. Blood and water poured from my hands and into the tub.

Water cannot wash them away.

The water rose past my waist and kneecaps.

Jesus, to that fountain of Thine.

It lapped at the side of the tub.

"Cleanse me by Thy washing divine.

In God there is power. Salvation.

Whiter than the snow.

Whiter than the snow.

Wash me in the blood of the Lamb.
And I shall be whiter than snow.

Water Bearers

Time moves slow since Daddy passed. Mama sits at the wooden desk in the bedroom they shared, writing in her journal and probably on her second pack of cigarettes for the day. I wonder about that journal a lot. She keeps it on her nightstand next to the worn-out Bible she barely opens.

"This is how I stay connected to my grandmama," she always says.

I peek through the door to ask if she is coming to church with us.

"Not this time baby," she responds without looking up from her journal.

Mama doesn't go to church much, but she makes me and my sisters go every Sunday. When I asked her why she makes us go since she doesn't, she replied calmly, "God can't do too much of nothing with me, but it's not too late for y'all."

I wasn't sure what she meant by that, but there was no arguing with Mama.

This morning I woke up as soon as the sun hit the window of the crowded bedroom I share with my two sisters. Our full-sized bed sits against the bare wall opposite an oversized window. Maye sleeps in the middle since she is the youngest, and Victoria sleeps on the side nearest to the wall. I sleep facing the window because I like the way the sun pulls me out of my sleep. After we're all up, I lay out our Sunday clothes. Today we have to sing in the children's choir so I decide to wear my favorite light purple linen dress that flares out a little at the knee and ties up in the back. Grandma Sarah bought it for my eleventh birthday a few months ago and I always wear it on special occasions.

Once we are dressed, we walk out to the peach tree behind our house to get a few for breakfast. With our peaches in hand and a few packed in a grocery bag in case we get hungry, we make our way up the wide dirt road toward church. The church is visible from our house. It sits on a steep hill next to a wooden sign that reads: *Still Valley M.B. Church.* The outside is all white and a tiny, black cross sits on the pointed part of the roof. It's very small compared to the white folks' church in the middle of town, resembling a castle with windows that remind me of a rainbow. I always want to see how it looks on the inside, but Mama said Black folks wasn't welcome there unless we were cooking or cleaning. When I asked her why, she laughed and said, "Cause they evil."

Our church looks much bigger on the inside. We have a kitchen where all the church ladies do the cooking every fourth Sunday, and a short hallway connecting the kitchen and the worship area that always smells like strong old lady perfume. There are two rows of pews on each side of the room with space in between for people to walk through. Me, Maye, and Victoria go directly to the choir stand with the other children. Once the congregation is settled and devotion is over, the choir director motions for us to stand up.

When the music starts I can already feel the energy shift in the room. Grandma Sarah, who sits on the front row with the other church mothers, stands up swaying and clapping her hands. Others in the church begin to stand as we belt out a fast-paced song we spent weeks practicing. I can see the hips of women swaying to the beat of the drums. Hands clapping and *Hallelujahs!* are now in sync with our voices. My heart is beating fast like my body got a hold of that spirit I see moving through the crowd. I feel a strong urge to start dancing and moving my feet to the beat, but I hold it in and keep singing. Once the song ends, the music slows down to give folks time to steady their bodies that are still trembling from catching the spirit, I spend the rest of service imagining how it would feel to move to the sound of drums like I watch the women in my church do every Sunday.

***

The smell of greens, fried chicken, and that rose perfume Grandma Sarah wears greets us at the door. Every Sunday evening we have supper at her house. Mama used to come with us, but her and Grandma Sarah haven't spoken since the day of Daddy's funeral. The night after Daddy's repast I overheard Grandma Sarah tell Mama she didn't need to spend too much time grieving.

"You got kids to tend to. Get yourself together," she had said.

That ended with Mama telling Grandma Sarah she wasn't welcome in our house anymore.

Still, Grandma Sarah wrapped up a plate for us to take home for her.

"Lee, grab that for your mama before y'all leave. I know she sittin' over there starvin' herself."

I nod and sit down at the table with her and my sisters to eat.

When it is nearing time for us to go home, we go into the living room and stand in a circle so Grandma Sarah can pray for us. Me, Victoria, and Maye grab hands as Grandma Sarah disappears into her bedroom. She comes back with a glass bottle that looks like perfume. This is her bottle of holy oil. She lights up the white candle next to a bowl of water on the living room table and places a black bible in the center. Next, she pours a little of the oil in her hand and dabs it in the shape of a circle on each of our foreheads, mumbling something I can never make out. The oil is warm on my head, and the smell reminds me of the frankincense candle Mama burns sometimes. This has been Grandma Sarah's Sunday ritual for as long as I can remember. Before Daddy died she used to say, "I got to keep y'all protected from all the hell James keepin' up down there." She was never too fond of Daddy, but she tolerated him. After our prayer, she kisses us good night and sends us home.

It is dark by the time we make it to our house, so I quickly run a bath for Maye and Victoria. Lately, I've had to help out more with the girls. Mama has been too sad to do anything but sit in her room, smoke cigarettes, and write in her journal. Once the girls are in bed, I tiptoe to Mama's room.

"What is it Lee?" I hear her say just before I make a fist to knock on the door.

"I was just coming to tell you good night and bring you this plate Grandma Sarah sent."

She motions for me to sit on the little chest at the foot of her bed and grabs the plate from me.

"What she talkin bout today?" she asks.

"Nothing really," I say.

That's Mama's way of asking about Grandma Sarah without seeming like she cares. She opens the plate and picks over some of it before handing it back to me.

"Put it in the 'fridgerator, I'll finish it tomorrow," she says.

As I get up to leave, she stands up, hugs me real tight. "I love you, okay? No matter what nobody say. I love you."

"I know, Mama," I say before heading to my room for bed.

***

I am floating in the middle of the ocean. The water is almost to my neck, and the coldness of it makes my body stiff. Mama is further out in the ocean with a helpless look on her face. As I swim closer to her I can see Daddy behind her, trying to pull her down into the ocean with him. She is screaming and telling me to go back. I am frantically trying to get to her, but the closer I swim the higher the waves get until I am completely under. I can feel my nose and mouth fill with water. As my body starts to give out, I feel hands on my shoulders.

I wake up with a scream caught in my throat and a wet face. This is the second time I've dreamt about the ocean since Daddy's funeral. Last time he was trying to pull me in, but I woke up just before my head went under. I turn over and peer out the window. The sun is just barely out. Maye and Victoria are sound asleep, and the house is eerily quiet. I walk into the kitchen to get a glass of water, and notice that Mama's bedroom light is still on. I want to check on her, but I don't. Instead, I go outside and sit on our porch swing. It hangs at the far end of our porch and makes a light squeaky sound as it moves back and forth. It is my favorite thing to do early in the morning while everyone is sleep. Daddy used to wake up early too, and come swing with me. He was mean sometimes, but wise. Gentle as he was rough. The last time we were out here he told me he was sorry. I asked him for what, and he replied almost as if something was stuck in his throat, "Everything." And then we just sat there in silence, breathing in the smell of pines trees and watching the sun come up from behind them. That evening Daddy would leave to go hunting, at least that's what he told Mama, and never return.

The day it happened, me and my sisters were sitting on the couch watching TV. There was a real loud knock at the door. I ran to tell Mama because we weren't allowed to answer the door after the sun goes down. When she opened the door it was Grandma Sarah and two of Daddy's friends. Grandma Sarah looked at us and then at her. They all walked back into Mama's bedroom and shut the door. It was quiet for a couple of minutes before Mama let out a long, melodic scream that made my insides shake. After that everything is a blur until the funeral. Maye and Victoria cried almost as much as Mama. I wanted to cry, but I couldn't. I didn't know what to make of his death. I didn't know what to make of death at all. Later that night after Grandma Sarah and Mama's argument,

I went into Mama's room and sat at the foot of her bed. She looked at me half smiling, half crying. I asked her how Daddy died, and she looked away from me and out her bedroom window.

"He was tired of living with himself, so he stopped," she said.

I wanted to ask her what that meant, but I tried to comfort her instead. Grandma Sarah would later tell me he went off into the woods and shot himself.

"A coward," she would say.

I'm surprised out of my thoughts by Maye who is peeking her tiny head out of the screen door. She comes over and plops herself into my lap to ask when I'm going to start getting ready for school. I get up to get us dressed before we wait outside for the bus.

Mama's light is still on.

With me and Victoria trailing behind her, Maye runs to the bedroom door yelling Mama's name.

"Come in," I hear her say.

We go in and Mama's eyes are swollen like she has been crying all night.

"What's wrong Mama?" Victoria asks, before plopping down on the bed to hug her.

Mama ignores her and slowly stands up, motioning us out of the room. She walks with us to the front door, giving us each a hug and kiss on our way out. The bus pulls up and Maye and Victoria rush excitedly to greet it. Mama's scent of lavender soap and cigarettes linger on my skin as I walk toward the bus. I watch her out the bus window as we pull off, standing in the screen door, staring blankly with a sideways smile.

***

Mama has become so lost in her own sadness. Victoria asks me if she still loves us.

"Of course she still love us," I say. "She just forgot how to show it."

Most days I'm just trying to keep myself and my sisters distracted from the grief that has nearly swallowed our house whole. Some nights I ask God to make things better. I'm not sure if he hears me, but I remember in church the pastor saying that we should talk to God like we would anybody. And so I speak to God throughout the day. "God, please make Mama happy again, and make her laugh like she used to."

I keep wondering if Mama has been talking to him, but I don't ask.

The sadder she gets, the more vivid the dreams become. I am always in the ocean, but Daddy and Mama are no longer there. Now there is a woman with long, thick black hair. The texture looks rough and kinky like mine. Her skin is real dark and smooth like Mama's, but she has Grandma Sarah's sand-colored eyes. In the dream, she is reaching out to me, but the closer I get to her the further back she appears. When I reach out to touch her, I wake up, cold and sweaty. Grandma Sarah says all dreams mean something.

"Sometimes God is tryin' to tell you something."

***

Grandma Sarah sits in her recliner looking through a big green book. She looks up and greets us with a smile as we walk in.

"Mama sent this food for you," I say.

She grins and takes the plate from me. Maye grabs the book from Grandma Sarah's lap.

"What's this Grandmama?"

"That's our family album," she says. "My mama gave it to me, and maybe one day before I leave this earth I'll give it to your mama if she act right."

She lets out a big laugh, like how Mama used to before she got sad. I pick up the green photo album and flip through it, stopping on a picture of a woman who looks too familiar.

"Grandma Sarah, who is this woman?"

"That's your Great-great grandmama, Emma Lee, my mama's mama. Your mama named you after her," she says.

"She looks like the lady in my dreams."

"Hmm...ain't that somethin'. What she say?"

"She ain't say nothin'. She just reach out her hand and then I wake up."

Grandma Sarah gives me strange look and raises out of her recliner. She leads us into her windowless prayer room that smells like cinnamon and burning wood. The walls are paneled with cedar like the rest of the house except black and white pictures of people I don't know hang on the walls. I spot the lady from my dreams in a picture that sits next to a large white cross. There is a picture of Grandma Sarah's mama right next to hers. In the middle of the room, there is a large quilt spread out on the floor. Grandma Sarah grabs the picture of Grandma Emma Lee and a shiny white bible with gold font from out of a small cabinet near the door.

She hands me the picture and the bible.

"Now listen here. Take this home, place the picture and the bible next to your bed. Sit you out a glass water and a small bowl of food if you can. Then say a prayer to her. If she visiting you, you need to find out what she want."

"What I need water and food for?"

"You can't ask for nothing without giving something. You got to give an offering, just like we do in church. Understand what I'm saying, baby?"

"Yes Ma'am, I understand."

"Now do as I say, and you'll get the answer you need."

***

I wake up the next morning to find our bedroom filled with water. Noticing that I'm in bed alone, I jump up in a panic. The water is freezing cold against my ankles. "Maye! Victoria! Where are y'all?" I yell their names frantically, walking into the living room which is now empty. I can feel the water creeping up to my knees. I run back to Mama's room to find Grandma Emma Lee standing in the doorway. Her long, thick, dark hair floats behind her in the water. She smiles at me.

Is this a dream? I think to myself.

"It's not a dream Lee. Didn't you call out for me?"

Her voice is soft and soothing like Mama's. Before I can answer her, I feel the water moving up my waist. She grabs my hand and leads me out the door. We step into an open body of water where our porch was supposed to be. The house disappears behind us. I feel my eyes getting warm.

"Where am I? Where is everybody?" I ask.

She looks back at me, smiling, and pulls me further into what looks like the ocean from my dreams. She points toward the mist that sits far out into the distance.

"Look," she says.

As we move closer, I see a group of women. The sunlight reflects off their dark black skin. They are dressed in long white dresses that drape easily over their bodies as they wade and dance through the water.

"These are your mothers. You can only help your mama if you look to them," she says.

I look at the women, and then back to her, but she is gone. The water rises up to my neck, and I can barely keep my face above it enough to breathe. I don't fight it this time. I let the water swallow my body. It grows more turbulent, jerking me back and forth, and I can feel the saltiness of it down my throat. The ocean abruptly settles as I slip away to the sounds of familiar voices calling out my name.

She (A retelling of *The Giving Tree*)

We must first establish that the Giving Tree, like all trees, is a she, and she loved her boy with all of her trunk, branches, and roots. The boy loved the tree in return. He swung from her branches, which she wrapped securely around him. His laughter rang through the summer air and gave her happiness far more sustaining than the sun beaming down or even the rain coming down from the sky. She gave him apples from her branches when he calmed down enough to be hungry. When he was tired, he lay at the base of her trunk and she covered him with her leaves so he would not catch a chill. She shaded him with her branches so that he would not get burned by the sun. When he would snore in his sleep, she would gently turn him over on his side so that he could breathe easier. She would listen to his quiet breathing and sigh happily the way trees do when they watch their boys sleep. She would smile the way trees do watching his freckled nose wrinkle.

One day the boy woke from his nap and pulled out a scouting knife. He flicked it open and he carved their initials into her trunk. Then he carved a heart around them. It hurt her, but the boy looked down and was pleased. The boy smiled and though it still stung, she was happy. The boy wrapped his arms around her trunk and squeezed as tight as he could. The tree wrapped her branches around the boy and she was so happy she cried with joy the way trees do.

One day the boy did not come bounding over the hill pigeon-toed, as he always did. He did not come the day after, either.

The tree was sad, but she knew it was only natural he go out in the world. So she waited for his return the way trees do. She worried for him. She paced the ways trees do, shivering and shaking, losing all of her shiny red apples, and all of her leaves turned the color of the sunset and fell to the ground. She extended her naked branches toward the sky and offered prayers for the boy: that he would return to her, that he would be safe, that he was happy out in the world.

Many years passed.

The boy returned. Now he was gangly and lean. He walked with a strut and his arm was thrown around the shoulder of a pretty girl with golden hair that sparkled as it flowed down her back. But the tree still recognized the boy from a distance as trees do. He still had the freckles scattered across his face, he still walked slightly pigeon-toed, and his smile was still crooked, pulling up a little more on the left than the right, looking like a mischievous smirk and warming her bark from the inside out.

The tree was happy. Blossoms bloomed fragrant on her branches. She smiled the way trees do when their boys return. She extended her branches so that he could swing in them once again. But he did not jump into them as he had done before. He stayed next to the girl with his hand wrapped around her waist. Then reached up and plucked a few blossoms from the tree and offered them to the girl. The boy and girl laid at the base of the tree holding hands. The tree spread her branches over them to shade them from the sun. The boy and girl slept, wrapped in each other's arms. And the tree looked down at them and smiled, the way trees do, because she was happy to add someone else to her family.

When the boy and girl woke, the boy pulled out his pocket knife and cut through the tree's initials and he carved the girl's initials right above the place he had carved the tree's. This was excruciating. But the boy looked at the girl and then back at his work and was pleased. So the tree smiled in the way trees do. Then the boy took the girl's hand and they ran back to the world.

The tree was alone once again.

The sun shone brightly, and the rain fell just the right amount, but the tree did not extend her branches for sustenance. Her leaves fell to the ground prematurely. Her apples did not get any bigger than acorns and they were hard, green, and bitter. These eventually fell to the ground. Not even the insects ate them. They simply sat on the ground between her roots until they rotted and joined the earth.

Many years passed.

The boy returned, but he was now a man. He was no longer gangly and his mischievous smile was now a lopsided frown. He drove up in a pickup truck that he parked next to her and jumped down. He was still pigeon-toed and at the memory of his little legs wrapped in her branches, she smiled. She reached out to him and asked him to swing in her branches so that he could be happy once again. She asked if he was hungry, for if he waited, she could grow him some apples to sustain him.

He tapped his foot impatiently. "Tree, you do not understand what it is like out there, I need to make a shelter for myself and for the woman so that we can start a family."

The tree smiled—an easy fix. "Please take my branches, beloved. Make a home for you and the woman so that you can be happy."

The man did not hesitate. He pulled a saw from the bed of the truck, climbed up her trunk, and started to cut down all of her branches. He threw them to the ground and when he had cut them all down, he gathered them up and threw them into the bed of the truck. The man did not say goodbye, he closed the door to the bed of the truck and simply said, "Thanks tree." Then he jumped into the truck and drove away.

The tree stood stripped. She had no branches to raise in prayer for the boy.

She waited. There was nothing else to do.

Many years passed. Then many more.

A day came when the man ran toward her with an axe. He was still pigeon-toed but he had less hair on his head and the hair that was left had started to turn grey. Though she had stood motionless for quite some time, waiting, she was happy. She smiled the best way she could without her branches.

It took the man some time to get to her. And when he arrived, he rested his hand on her trunk as he caught his breath, the axe rested on the ground between them. She told him, "Please come sit against my trunk so that you can catch your breath and be happy."

The man stood straight once he had caught his breath and he said, "Tree, you do not know how it is out there. How much pressure there is. How much you must give. I must escape. Give me your trunk so that I can leave this place for a while.

The tree hesitated.

The man pointed to the carved heart that both of their initials had once been in together, before he had scratched out her initials with his knife. "Tree, don't you remember you loved me? Don't you remember the happy times we shared?"

The tree saw in her memory his face, placid and content beneath her branches. She remembered turning the boy over in his sleep so that he could breathe easier, she remembered the feeling of his arms wrapped around her trunk as far as they could reach.

She sighed. "Please take my trunk and sail away so that you can be happy."

The boy picked up the axe off of the ground and he cut down her trunk. The tree was surprised at how quickly he was able to do it, but he did.

The tree had no idea how he took the trunk away as she could no longer see.

She waited. She felt the sun on her stump. She felt snow land on her stump and then melt. She felt little feet, big feet, bird feet, and beast feet. But none of them were the man. She heard birds singing. Deer eating grass. Moss grew on top of her. A family of termites found a home in her. A squirrel hid its treasures in a hole at the base of her stump. Things were good and the tree started to remember what happiness felt like. Then she heard a song. She called out, "Who is there?"

There was laughter and the feeling of a branch brushing her stump. "Grandmother tree we are your granddaughters, we sing to you so that you will not be lonely. We have seen you give everything and now we want you to rest and be happy."

And the tree was happy. She listened to her granddaughters' songs and their daughters' as well.

One day, the man returned. She recognized his footsteps though she could not see him, because a tree always recognizes her boy. He stood in front of her stump. She asked him, "Son what can I give you. You see I have nothing left to give."

The man sighed. "Tree, you do not know what it is like out there for an old man. They forget about you. They leave you alone in a forgotten place and never return."

The tree did not hesitate. "Please my son, come sit on my stump. Rest your bones so that you can be happy."

The man sat and the tree could not see whether he smiled, but she was happy anyway.

Bios

Stephanie Avery has a lifestyle blog that focuses on self-care. She currently attends SCAD as a writing major, where she started incorporating the southern dialect into her writing. Her biggest inspiration for this story was *The Color Purple*.

rebekah blake, also published under Rebekah Coxwell, is currently an English teacher in Suffolk County. She has an upcoming novel, *Falling*, coming out with SFK publishing. The ARCs are available now and the book will be officially released, Fall 2021. She lives with her babies and the only plant she's been able to keep alive, Basil.

Danielle Buckingham is a Black Southern writer from Louisville, Mississippi. She has work published or forthcoming in the New Orleans Review, Raising Mothers, Black Stew, and elsewhere.

Emily Capers lives in Chicago where she recently earned an MFA in Fiction. Her writing explores the varieties of her identity while creating a voice for herself in the time of social movements that are important to her. Her work has appeared in Allegory Ridge, High Shelf Press, and The Mill.

Melie Ekunno is a Senior Chemistry and English double major. She grew up in Abuja, Nigeria—the city where her love for literature began. She credits her full recovery from a lifelong addiction to novels to the impossible schedule she currently maintains at St. Olaf College. On a good day, you may spot her ridiculous Afro-puffs (space buns) from miles away; she maintains that they are a symbol of her commitment to not growing up anytime soon.

Martins Favour is a writer and a believer in all the beautiful things life affords us. Her works have appeared in Kalahari Review, African writers and other relatively remote platforms. When she's not writing however, she lives out her not-so-big dreams in her head.

Wandeka Gayle is a Jamaican writer, visual artist, and Assistant Professor of Creative Writing at Spelman College. She has a PhD in English/Creative Writing from the University of Louisiana at Lafayette and has received writing fellowships from Kimbilio Fiction, Callaloo Creative Writing Workshop, The Hurston/Wright Foundation, and Martha's Vineyard Institute of Creative Writing. She is the author of *Motherland and Other Stories* (Peepal Tree Press 2020).

Ashanti Hardy is a writer and teacher from Atlanta, GA. She has always enjoyed writing that captures the complexity of people. Her energy to write comes from a quote by Toni Morrison: "If there's a book that you want to read, but it hasn't been written yet, then you must write it."

Amani-Nzinga Jabbar is the author of the novel, *I Bear Witness*, and a professor of English. She resides in Atlanta.

Adrian Joseph is a writer, photographer, and performance artist from Jeanerette, Louisiana. She specializes in conceptualization through poetry and sound and holds a B.A. in Sociology from the University of Louisiana at Lafayette. Her work has been previously published in Nia magazine. For more, follow her on Instagram @adrisoartsy.

Desi Lenc's fiction is steeped in surrealism, while her non-fiction is rooted in the tangible solutions non-profits and sustainable businesses provide. Her blog, Outcast's Mag, celebrates the unique contributions artists, eco-friendly business owners, and non-profits offer to their communities. She's currently working on her first novel, which you can find an excerpt of in the upcoming anthology, *New Transmissions From The Dark Fantastic Continuum*.

Melissa A. Matthews is an artist, writer, entrepreneur, and first generation American of Afro-Trinidadian descent that was born and raised in Brooklyn, NY. She currently lives and works in her cultural home of Trinidad & Tobago. Her writing explores the duality of her citizenship as an American who is not very American and a Trinidadian who is not very Trinidadian. You can find her @mamltdart on Instagram and on

Medium.com @melissamatthews_37885.

Adaora Raji earned a Bachelor of Arts degree in Broadcast Journalism from the University of Benin, Nigeria. Her fiction has appeared or is forthcoming in Arlington Literary Journal, the Coachella Review and the Bookends Review. Her poem, "The day you unwrap happiness," is a finalist in the 2020 Loving Gaze Poetry Contest.

Leslie D. Rose is a Jersey-born, D.C. Metro based veteran journalist, editor, photographer, and poet. She is the founder and chief operating officer of the independent consulting firm/creative activism organization, CreActiv, LLC, co-founder of Black Out Loud Conference, LLC, and the copy/weekend editor at Blavity News. Leslie is also a lipstick aficionado, Babyface superfan, loving cat mother, and her whole Afro-Rican self at all times. She holds a B.A. in mass communication with a minor in creative writing from Xavier University of Louisiana and is #HBCUProud. Leslie's work has been published and featured on various outlets, including Passages North, Indiefeed, and All Def Poetry. She is the author of the full-length journalism-inspired book of poetry, *The Newsroom*. She also has four research papers published in *The St. James Encyclopedia of Hip Hop Culture*, 1st Edition (2018, Gale/St. James Press).

Theresa Sylvester is a Zambian fiction author based in Australia. Her short story, "Rootless" will be published in Black Warrior Review's next issue. Notable works include "Atonement" which placed third in the Notes From Lusaka Short Story Prize 2020, "Figures in the fire" in the Rockingham Writers Centre 2019 Anthology in Perth, Australia, and "Cracked Flowerpots" published online by midnight & indigo. When she isn't mothering and 'wifing,' Theresa attends writing workshops and loiters in libraries and bookshops.

About The Editor

Ianna A. Small is the founder of midnight & indigo Publishing and creator of *midnight & indigo*, a literary platform dedicated to short stories and narrative essays by Black women writers. m&i is her love letter to Black women like herself, who long to reach the pinnacle of their purpose. As the executive editor of midnight & indigo, she oversees editorial and creative direction for the digital and print platforms. A media marketing executive, Ms. Small also has 20+ years of experience developing partnerships, distribution, and content marketing initiatives for entertainment brands including BET, Disney Channel, ESPN, ABC, FX, VH1, MTV, HOT97, and more.

An avid fan of Black and South Asian literature, Korean horror, and all things Jesus + Michelle Obama + The Golden Girls + cultural food documentaries, she dreams of one day running midnight & indigo from a lounge chair overlooking the archipelagos of her happy place, Santorini.

Ms. Small is a proud graduate of Syracuse University and active member of ACES: The Society for Editing and the EFA (Editorial Freelancers Organization). She is a granddaughter to Irma, daughter to Nadia, and mother of Jalen Anthony, who is simply: her reason.

CPSIA information can be obtained
at www.ICGtesting.com
Printed in the USA
LVHW110726020821
694295LV00001B/24

9 781732 891784